# "TESS, COME HERE QUICK!"

His sudden urgency made Tess run. Curt stepped out of the doorway and leaned against the wall.

Sherwood Draper lay on the floor, his face turned toward the door. His eyes were closed. A circle of wet, fresh blood soaked the back of his corduroy jacket. One blade of a pair of large shears were buried to the hilt in the center of the bloody circle.

"He's still alive!" Tess said urgently. She pressed two fingers against Draper's neck and felt a faint, erratic pulse. His eyes opened.

"Who did this to you, Professor?"

He whispered something . . . and then, as Tess watched, the light went out of his eyes, and the faint pulse beneath her fingers stopped.

*Other Iris House Mysteries by*
**Jean Hager**
*from Avon Books*

BLOOMING MURDER
DEAD AND BURIED
DEATH ON THE DRUNKARD'S PATH

# THE
# *Last Noel*

## AN IRIS HOUSE B&B MYSTERY

# JEAN HAGER

AVON BOOKS ◆ NEW YORK

AVON BOOKS
A division of
The Hearst Corporation
1350 Avenue of the Americas
New York, New York 10019

Copyright © 1997 by Jean Hager
Published by arrangement with the author
Visit our website at http://www.AvonBooks.com
Library of Congress Catalog Card Number: 97-93748
ISBN: 0-380-78637-0

First Avon Books Printing: December 1997

AVON TRADEMARK REG. U.S. PAT. OFF. AND IN OTHER COUNTRIES, MARCA REGISTRADA, HECHO EN U.S.A.

Printed in the U.S.A.

WCD 10  9  8  7  6  5  4  3

The author wishes to thank
Kathy Thirtyacre Person for the title.

# Chapter 1

"You're the last person I expected to stab me in the back, Tess Darcy!" stormed Claire Chandler as soon as the phone was picked up, without even giving Tess a chance to say hello.

"Claire?"

"I thought you were my friend!"

"Of course I'm your friend, Claire." Tess grimaced at Luke, who was sprawled on her sofa, eating the last of the popcorn and watching the late television news. Tess's gray Persian, Primrose, dozed, curled beside him. Primrose had only recently deigned to acknowledge Luke Fredrik's presence in Tess's life, and Luke said he'd been better off when Primrose hated him. Now, he complained, every pair of trousers he owned was covered with cat hairs.

Luke glanced up when he heard the caller's name. Tess made a throat-slitting motion. He held up both hands as if to ward off a blow and mouthed a silent, "You're on your own."

It was 10:20 on the night of Monday, December 5, and the TV weather man was saying, "Get out your flannel jammies and put an extra blanket on the bed tonight, folks. Tomorrow most of western Missouri will wake up to six to eight inches of snow."

1

Claire Chandler's strident voice sliced into Tess's distracted attention and brought it back to her grievance. "Then why did you leave that message on my machine?" she demanded.

"I wanted to tell you in person, Claire, but I had to drive to Springfield this afternoon and I didn't want you to hear it from someone else," Tess fibbed glibly. She would rather Claire have heard it from *anyone* else.

"Who on earth is Sherwood Draper?"

Tess glanced at her ceiling, toward the second floor where the interloper himself and his wife, Mavis, were already settled in the Darcy Flame Suite. Tess had a handful of bookings for January and February, but the tourist season wouldn't really get back into gear until mid-March. At the moment, the Drapers were the only paying guests in residence at Iris House—though not the only guests. Also in residence were Tess's young half-brother, Curt, and half-sister, Madison, whom she'd picked up at the Springfield-Branson airport that afternoon.

It had not been the happy reunion Tess had envisioned. Exhausted from the long flight from Paris, thirteen-year-old Curt had been staggering and dazed from jet leg, but was as friendly as a puppy, a very pooped puppy. Fourteen-year-old Madison, who appeared more rested, seemed to be pouting. After several miles, Tess had given up trying to engage Madison in conversation. Back in Victoria Springs, she had delivered her siblings to her Aunt Dahlia's house for dinner. Dahlia had brought them back to Iris House at nine. By then, they were asleep on their feet and had immediately gone to bed.

"I understand Draper is from a small town east of Denver," Tess said in answer to Claire's question. "I can't remember the name of the town, but he's supposed to have had a lot of experience directing Christmas pageants."

"*I've* had a lot of experience." Claire Chandler was the unpaid and self-appointed social director for the Community Church and head of the women's ministry committee. A virtual dynamo, she organized an elaborate Adventure Week for the kids each summer, which included crafts, swimming, and field trips in addition to Bible lessons. Claire had also planned and directed the church's Christmas programs for years. But they had a progressive young minister now who had new ideas.

"I know you've had extensive experience, Claire. And I'm terribly sorry about all this, but Draper was on the way here before I even knew he was coming. Believe me, I was as shocked as you are." Darned if she would take the blame for something she'd had no hand in. "Pastor Matt called me about noon and asked me to let you know before tomorrow's practice."

In a weak moment, over a month ago, Tess had volunteered to help behind the scenes at the pageant. Reverend Sandifer, or Pastor Matt as he preferred to be called, had promptly made her his assistant—in other words, he'd put her in charge of the scut work. Which seemed to include handling all the chores that nobody else wanted, like delivering unpleasant news. When Pastor Matt called and dropped the bomb about bringing in an experienced outsider as pageant director, he'd also reserved the Darcy Flame suite for the Drapers. Having the Drapers in the most expensive accommodations in Iris House was Tess's reward for delivering the news to Claire.

Tess had tried to turn down the assignment, but Pastor Matt had refused to take her seriously, mumbling over the phone that his secretary had the afternoon off and he was already late for his Kiwanis Club meeting. Then he'd hung up.

Of course, the pastor had known exactly how Claire would react to this invasion of her turf.

"I've never heard of this Draper person, Tess," Claire persisted.

"Nor had I, until today."

"Pastor Matt must have known Draper before he moved to Victoria Springs," Claire surmised.

"I don't think so. I believe Draper was recommended

by Lily—'' Tess could have bitten her tongue. She knew the moment Lily's name left her mouth that it was a mistake. Claire and Lily were in a perpetual power struggle over who was in charge of various church social functions. Since Claire had been there longer, she usually got her way, but Lily made an occasional inroad.

In this case, instead of a mere inroad, Lily had plowed a regular six-laner through Claire's domain.

''*Lily Brookside!* That conniving little sneak! I might have known she was behind this.''

Too late, Tess tried to backpedal. ''I shouldn't have said that, Claire. I can't actually swear it was Lily. I didn't personally hear her talk to Pastor Matt about Draper.''

''Of course it was Lily,'' Claire snapped. ''It's just like her. She probably thinks this Draper person will show me up by putting on a better pageant than the ones we've had in the past, the ones I've *slaved* over with no thought of remuneration or even gratitude. Why, I've given my *life* to that church!''

''I'm sure the congregation appreciates it, too, Claire,'' Tess said weakly.

''I'll bet they didn't get this Draper person for free!''

''I wouldn't know about that,'' Tess demurred, though of course Claire must be right. ''But as for besting our past pageants, I really don't see how that's possible. Everyone says they'd swear last year's production was professionally produced, if they didn't know otherwise.''

Luke cocked an eyebrow at Tess's shameless flattery. She ignored him, then smiled fleetingly as Primrose stretched and began to sharpen her claws on Luke's knee. Luke winced, lifted the cat off him and set her on the floor. Primrose slitted her yellow eyes at him, flipped her fluffy tail, and padded over to weave in and out between Tess's legs.

Claire was not the least bit mollified by Tess's flattery. ''So Lily recommended this Sherwood Draper to Pastor Matt?'' she asked thoughtfully.

Tess might as well tell her all she knew. She'd never

convince her Lily wasn't behind it now. "I heard the Brooksides met the Drapers last winter. I believe it was while they were staying at the same ski lodge in Vail."

"Oh, the ski trip." Claire sounded thoughtful. "Denny didn't want to go on that trip, you know, but Lily wheedled until she got her way. She's good at that." There was a pause, presumably for Tess to add to the list of Lily's flaws. She declined.

"Poor Denny," Claire said after a few moments of silence. "Can you see him on skis?"

It *was* a comical idea. Tess suppressed a chuckle. "I never thought about it."

"Well, I have, and I'm sure he sat in the lodge while Lily did her thing." She emphasized the last two words, but Tess pretended not to take her meaning. Lily did like to flirt, but Tess had always assumed Lily wasn't serious and would never actually have an extramarital affair. Of course, she didn't know Lily well enough to swear to that. As for Denny Brookside, Lily's husband, he was fifteen or sixteen years older than his wife and disliked socializing, even eating out. It drove Lily crazy. Since Lily did not strike Tess as particularly spiritual, Tess had long suspected she involved herself in church activities merely to have an excuse to get out of the house.

"I'm sorry I yelled at you, Tess," Claire said. "This is not your fault. I can see that now."

"I'm sure Draper will be happy to have you work with him," Tess offered, not at all sure. From what she had seen of Sherwood Draper when the Drapers checked in earlier that evening, he was pretty full of himself.

Claire snorted. "Well, I'm not sure I want to work with *him*. But thank you for letting me know what Lily's been up to, Tess."

"As I said, Claire, I can't swear—"

"Oh, never mind. I won't tell Lily where I heard it. I'll see you tomorrow at practice."

Tess hung up. "At least she's not blaming me anymore," she said as she returned to the sofa and flopped down beside Luke. Primrose leaped into her lap and curled up, purring. Stroking the cat's soft fur, Tess settled her head on Luke's shoulder to watch the last few minutes of the news broadcast, but she was too distracted now to focus on what the newscaster was saying.

"Sounded like she's transferred her anger to Lily Brookside."

Worried, Tess chewed her bottom lip. "I wish I hadn't mentioned Lily's name. I hope she and Claire don't have words at the church tomorrow."

Luke chuckled. "Dream on, sweetheart. Claire's not one to suffer slights in silence."

Tess sighed. "You're a big help."

"Just want you to be prepared."

"I hope Blanche has been forewarned," Tess said. "Maybe she can head Claire off, calm her down before she confronts Lily." Blanche Tandy was the church secretary, adept at mediating disagreements between church members and deflecting ire from the minister.

"If anybody can, it's Blanche," Luke agreed. "The woman could have made a fortune as a union mediator. Don't worry about it, honey. Let Blanche handle it."

Good advice, Tess told herself. Blanche had plenty of experience in making peace—she'd been the church secretary for twelve years, ever since she and her husband, Mike, moved to Victoria Springs. Mike managed a local hardware store and sang bass in the church choir. The Tandys' only child had died in infancy, which was certainly the most devastating thing that had ever happened to Blanche, and Tess suspected Blanche still wasn't over the loss. She had seen the longing looks Blanche cast at other people's babies, the melancholy in her eyes when she held them.

A few months ago, the Tandys had taken in a foster child—teenager, actually—Eddie Zoller, who, for the past year, had worked at the hardware store holidays and Saturdays. Eddie's mother was dead and his father, when he was around at all, stayed drunk most of the time. Although the man used to disappear for days, he always returned. But when Eddie moved in with the Tandys, his father left town in a huff, swearing that Victoria Springs had seen the last of *him*. Frankly, most of the townspeople hoped he spoke the truth. So far, he'd not returned and Tess doubted that Eddie had heard from his father since he went away.

At any rate, Blanche now had an outlet for her mothering instincts, albeit for a teenager who'd grown up with little supervision. Remembering Eddie's background, Tess wondered how the Tandys and the boy were getting along.

But she had more pressing matters to worry about now, she thought, remembering Curt, who was upstairs in the Arctic Fancy Room, and Madison, who slept right down the hall in Tess's spare bedroom. Frank Darcy, Tess's father, had been posted to foreign embassies ever since Curt and Madison were six and seven. They'd lived in Paris for the past five years, and Tess only saw them once a year, usually at Christmas. She had been expecting the whole family to arrive on December 22, until her father had phoned last week. He had to go to Greece, an unexpected business trip, and, since there would be several social functions, as well, he wanted to take Zelda with him. (Zelda, young as she was when Frank married her, had become a skilled diplomat's wife.) The children would be bored, so he wanted to send them to Victoria Springs early. He and Zelda would join them on the twenty-second, as planned.

Of course, Tess had agreed. She'd welcomed the chance to get to know Curt and Madison better, even though she wondered how she would entertain two teenagers. She'd actually had butterflies in her stomach when she met their plane and had tried valiantly to remain cheerful on the drive home from the airport that afternoon. The sparkling three-way conversation Tess had imagined turned out to be a sporadic one with Curt, who gamely answered her questions between dropping off for catnaps. Madison's responses, if you could call them that, were mumbled monosyllables. Plainly, she hadn't wanted to come to Victoria Springs early. For what reason, Tess didn't know. She only hoped Madison was in a better mood tomorrow. The thought of trying to entertain two amenable teenagers was bad enough, but dealing with a sullen, uncooperative fourteen-year-old girl for more than two weeks until her parents arrived filled Tess with trepidation.

The newscast ended and Luke lifted the remote control to turn off the TV. Then he gathered Tess into his arms. "If I stay the night, maybe we'll be snowed in tomorrow," he murmured against her hair. "Wouldn't that be fun?"

Tess sat up. "Oh, joy."

He leaned over and kissed her ear. "Do I detect a note of sarcasm?"

Tess grinned. "Whatever gave you that idea? Being snowed in with two teenagers is my dream, all right."

"Oh." He made a sour face. "I forgot about our little chaperones." He added after a moment, "You know, if we were married these problems wouldn't arise." From his crooked smile, Tess couldn't tell how serious he was. Luke had mentioned the *m* word before, but always in a teasing way. Thus far, Tess had managed to deflect a serious conversation on the subject.

He grunted as he got to his feet, pulling Tess up with him. He cocked his head, looking down at her, a lock of blond hair falling across his forehead, his sexy blue eyes softening. "I'm glad they're here, sweetheart, but they do live in Paris. They probably wouldn't turn a hair if I was still around in the morning."

Tess was sorely tempted, but opted for delayed gratification. "A free-wheeling lifestyle may be the thing in Paris," Tess said. "I wouldn't know, but I do know Zelda."

"Strict, huh?"

Tess nodded. "From what I've heard, she keeps Curt and Madison on a short rein. They attend a rigorous private school. The students are mostly the children of Americans living in Paris. From what Zelda says, none of the parents would want to put their kids in an American public school. Zelda says there's no discipline.''

"Does Zelda always indulge in sweeping generalizations?''

"I wondered about that myself. I suppose she reads about gang violence and thinks it happens in all American schools.''

"Maybe.'' Luke pulled her against him. "But enough about your stepmother.'' His arms tightened around her as he kissed her slowly.

She sighed dreamily when he lifted his head. Then she gave him an apologetic smile. "Later.''

"I'll hold that thought. If it snows, I'll pick you up for pageant practice tomorrow.'' Luke had volunteered to play a part in the drama. "I'll borrow Sidney's Jeep. I doubt the city will have all the streets plowed and sanded by then.'' Sidney Lawson was Luke's new assistant. Sidney had recently graduated from the University of Missouri and wanted to learn the investment business from a "master.'' Luke, who had managed an average twenty percent return on his clients' portfolios the last five years and consequently been written up in several financial publications, was Sidney's idol.

"Maybe the pastor will call off practice,'' Tess said hopefully.

"Don't count on it. Time's getting short. I'll be here about ten.''

"Isn't the market trading tomorrow?'' Tess asked. Luke kept an eagle eye on the stock, bond, and commodities markets from an office in his home, where he was connected to Wall Street via computer, fax machine, and telephone.

"I'll bring my cell phone and Sidney can transfer any important calls to me at the church.''

Tess had no doubt that Luke could work calmly amidst whatever chaos developed at the church. He was the most go-with-the-flow man she'd ever known. "Good," she said. "After hearing the weather forecast, I was dreading the drive. What would I do without you?"

He gave her a long look, then kissed her again. Shrugging into his down jacket, he said, "That would be a dire fate, woman."

"Indeed it would."

He winked broadly. "Just keep it in mind."

She walked with him to the door. After he'd gone, Tess wondered if he'd meant that last remark as a good-natured warning. But she was too tired to think about it and shrugged it off.

# Chapter 2

Mavis Draper couldn't sleep. She was weary after the drive to Victoria Springs, but for the past hour she had stared at the shadow of the canopy over the bed, feeling as tense as a tight-drawn rubber band. She had tried counting backward from a hundred, imagining peaceful scenes, consciously relaxing her body parts, one by one, starting with her toes and moving up. Nothing worked.

Beside her, Sherwood snored, sprawled on his back, his head turned toward a swag-draped window of the Darcy Flame Suite, arms flung to each side, the left resting like an iron bar across her mid-section. Her husband's snoring usually didn't keep her awake, but tonight she was acutely aware of every slight sound. She found herself counting the seconds between snores. Her irritation with Sherwood's ability to sleep any time, anywhere, grew with every clicking, snuffling snort as each wheezing breath in was followed by the little popping puff of air as he exhaled.

Sounded like a hog rooting in slop.

She'd already tried punching him twice and telling him to turn over, which he did, but the snoring resumed seconds later when he flopped on his back again. Finally, with a moan of defeat, she shoved

11

her husband's arm off her stomach and climbed out of bed.

Leaving the bedroom, she closed the door behind her and flipped on the light, revealing a large bathroom with brass faucets. Big, thick coral-colored towels were folded across brass racks. On one side of the room was a square, ivory jacuzzi and on the other, a generous-sized stall shower. The wallpaper matched the canopy and draperies in the bedroom—ivory background with a scattering of bright coral roses, the same color as the Darcy Flame Iris depicted in a gilt-framed painting in the sitting room.

The suite was, by far, the most elegant accommodations she'd ever stayed in. Sadly, she was in no mood to appreciate her surroundings. Digging her bare toes into the soft pile of the ivory carpet, she braced herself with both hands on the rim of the ivory wash basin. Leaning forward, she squinted nearsightedly at the reflection of her pinched, pale face. The light blue eyes were bloodshot, the lashes so blond they were virtually invisible. Fine blond hair frizzed around her face like hundreds of tiny springs. She looked like a cartoon character who'd just stuck her finger in a light socket.

She grimaced, revealing a gap between her two front teeth. Eighteen years ago, when they married, Sherwood had said he found the gap sexy. Remembering that, she felt a painful tightening in her stomach. Unfortunately, Sherwood didn't seem to find anything about her sexy these days. Impotency had invaded her marriage bed—it had been an unwelcome guest for almost a year now.

She had remained outwardly understanding and sympathetic, exactly as all the women's magazines advised, but inside alarm burgeoned. Now the alarm was generously laced with anger because Sherwood's ''problem'' seemed to manifest itself only with his wife. Just last summer he'd had a fling with one of his students at the junior college where he headed the speech and drama department. Mavis had followed him one night when he met the girl at a sleazy motel. Obviously, his sexual prowess had magically returned. To make the whole disgusting business even worse, the girl reminded Mavis of herself at nineteen—petite, blond, vulnerable, and dazzled by Sherwood Draper. How well she remembered that Sherwood could seem incredibly sophisticated and urbane to a naive teenager.

Two nights later, when she'd attempted to initiate sex, Sherwood had turned away, murmuring that it was no use, that he was too embarrassed and depressed even to talk about it. He knew she'd understand, she was so patient. He'd given her a brotherly pat on the thigh. She'd wanted to return the gesture with a slap.

Instead, she'd gone to his office, picking a time when she knew he would be in class. Engaging the secretary in conversation, she'd learned the name of the student by describing her, saying that she'd seen her on campus and thought she looked familiar. "Too bad you weren't here a half-hour earlier," the secretary said. "The girl came in to talk to professor Draper." She added pointedly, "She comes in a lot."

When the secretary left for a break, Mavis had extracted the cute blond student's name and home address from the computer. Then she'd written the girl's parents an anonymous note informing them that their daughter was having an affair with one of her teachers who, by the way, was married. The girl had not returned for the fall term.

Since August, Mavis was sure there had been no other women. She knew all the signs—Sherwood coming home with new clothes, more frequent visits with his hair stylist, a sudden increase in late "meetings" at the college. None of that had happened since his little blond squeeze went home. Mavis had begun to breathe easier.

Then Sherwood had received that phone call from the minister of the Community Church in Victoria Springs, Missouri, offering to pay all expenses and a generous stipend if Sherwood would come, as soon as classes ended, and direct the church's Christmas pageant. When Sherwood said, "Victoria Springs, Missouri? Exactly where is that?'' alarm bells had clanged in Mavis's head.

She hadn't heard the other end of the conversation, and Sherwood had not mentioned Lily Brookside's name, but Mavis knew, with the instinct of a wife whose husband played around, that Lily was behind the invitation. When he hung up, she'd asked, ''What kind of church is it?''

''According to the minister, a nondenominational Christian fellowship—whatever that means.''

Mavis didn't really care what it meant. She was only interested in where the church was located. ''Lily and Denny Brookside live in Victoria Springs, don't they?''

He'd looked innocently quizzical. ''Who?''

''That couple we met at the ski lodge,'' Mavis said between gritted teeth. ''They said they lived in Victoria Springs.''

''Did they? You know, I don't remember.''

She could always tell when Sherwood was lying. He got that little tic in his left eyelid.

He rubbed his left eye and gave a careless shrug. ''Oh, well, I'm sure they don't attend that church.''

Ha! And hounds don't wallow in manure piles.

When Mavis and Sherwood had met the Brooksides last winter in Vail, Mavis had immediately recognized that unmistakable light burning in Lily's eyes when she fixed them on Sherwood, a woman clearly hungering for a man. As for Lily's husband, Denny, he'd appeared bored and resigned to getting through the week without ever leaving the lodge. Much of the time he'd stayed in the Brooksides' room, reading, and the two Brookside teenagers had hooked up with a group of young people staying at the lodge. Lily had ''accidentally'' bumped into the Drapers a couple of times as they left the lodge. Thereafter, she assumed she was welcome to join them on the slopes and, half the time, for meals.

Occasionally Lily's husband bestirred himself to come out and take a meal with them, but more often he ordered from room service. Mavis thought the Brooksides had an odd marriage.

While in Vail, Mavis had made it her business to dog Sherwood's footsteps until they left for home. She was sure the attraction between her husband and Lily Brookside had not gone beyond a light-hearted holiday flirtation.

But now they would be on Lily's home ground for more than two weeks. It would be difficult to keep an eye on Sherwood for that long. Pretending to have her best interest at heart, he had suggested that she needn't accompany him to Victoria Springs—after all, it would only be dreary and boring for her and she must still have Christmas shopping to do. Any other time, he wouldn't even think of accepting the invitation, but she knew how much they needed the extra money for Christmas bills.

Mavis had assured him that her shopping was finished and she had no intention of spending the weeks preceding Christmas alone. She would assist with the pageant. No matter what happened in Victoria Springs, she'd rather be there than at home, wondering what her husband was up to, imagining Sherwood and the tall, attractive Lily Brookside together while Lily's husband had his head buried in a book.

Mentally, Mavis girded her loins for battle. In the morning, she would take extra care with her curling iron and makeup. She would wear the new rose tunic sweater with her black stirrup pants and black boots—the outfit made her look taller and somehow fashion-conscious. She knew she couldn't compete with Lily Brookside when it came to style, but she was determined that Sherwood wouldn't be ashamed of her appearance.

Her thoughts brought her up short. Ashamed? She had always been a good wife. Sherwood had no reason to be ashamed of her, and if he was, well, wasn't that his problem?

If only she could let it go at that!

But, no. Thanks to Lily, instead of her usual enjoyment in preparing for Christmas, Mavis would be anxiously trying to keep track of her husband and another woman.

The entire holiday season was spoiled, because of Lily.

Mavis despised the woman so much she was nearly sick with it. Why did every restless woman in the vicinity of her husband home in on Sherwood? Evidently he gave off some kind of man-on-the-prowl vibes.

Turning away from the mirror, Mavis left the bathroom. Sherwood's snores continued unabated. Her husband might be planning a romantic interlude with Lily Brookside but, clearly, his conscience was undisturbed. Sometimes she wondered if Sherwood even had a conscience.

She slid her feet into her furry white scuffs, drew her velour robe about her, and left the bedroom to prowl restlessly around the sitting room, skirting the coral sofa and ivory slipper chairs, resentment curling into a hot, hard ball lodged just beneath her breastbone.

Across town, in a long, low, ranch-style house, Denny Brookside fought his own battle with sleep. The barbecued pork ribs he'd eaten for dinner had given him heartburn. After over an hour of tossing and turning, he'd gotten up to keep from disturbing Lily and had taken more antacid tablets. Finally, the heartburn had eased, but he still wasn't sleepy.

He had gone into the den to read one of the two novels he'd picked up at the Queen Street Bookshop on his way home from work that afternoon. One was a courtroom drama, the other a futuristic thriller. He settled into his easy chair near the fireplace, where he could still feel warmth from the ashes of the hackberry logs they'd burned earlier in the evening. A seven-foot-tall pine tree covered with red and gold ornaments, lavish velvet bows and streamers, and blinking red lights took up one corner of the den. Lily always went ga-ga over Christmas and liked to get the tree up early.

Lily and the twins had decorated the tree last night, while Denny watched, a book open on his lap. Years ago, he'd given up touching the tree, beyond setting it up and making sure it was solidly anchored in its stand, because

Lily would reposition every ball and bow he hung. She said he had no sense of symmetry.

He picked up the two books to read the blurbs on their covers. Denny read two or three books a week. Lily accused him of escaping from real life into fiction, and she was probably right. It was funny because he'd read as little as possible while he was in school. He'd been a jock all through high school and college and had had hopes of being drafted by the pros—until he injured his knee in the last football game of his senior year. It had taken two surgeries to repair it well enough to bear his weight, and the knee still ached when the humidity was high. His body had been two hundred pounds of hard, lean muscle then. Now he weighed two-fifty and the muscles had softened from rock to mush.

He'd worked at staying fit for a long time after leaving college. In those days, which seemed like another lifetime now, he'd attracted women like flies and had dated so many of them that he could no longer remember all their names and faces. But he hadn't wanted to settle down until he met Lily, who was sixteen years his junior. After a brief courtship, he'd gotten up the courage to propose and, to his delight, she'd said yes. By that time, Denny never wanted to see another bar or fancy restaurant or attend another cocktail party again. He was partied out. He used his savings to buy a grocery store in Victoria Springs. He'd wanted nothing more than to make a home with Lily and start a family.

Those first few years of marriage had been the happiest of his life and then, seventeen years ago, the twins had come along. He'd wanted kids and he loved Boyd and Brenda, but they had sure put a strain on the marriage. For years, Lily's life had revolved around them. Denny, conscious of his responsibility to support the family and educate two children, spent more and more time at the store which had slowly expanded into one of the town's busiest supermarkets. Before long, his fitness program got squeezed out. He had to hurry home from the store every day to see the kids before Lily put them to bed. He just hadn't had time to go to the gym any more.

No longer could he use that excuse, but he couldn't seem to get motivated to start exercising again. He glanced down at his stomach, which protruded like a huge blob of dough over his jockey briefs. Disgusted, he pulled his robe together to cover the bulge.

Sometimes he fantasized about what his life would have been like if he hadn't busted his knee. If he'd made a name for himself in the pros, gotten some endorsements, invested wisely, he would be sitting pretty now instead of running a grocery store. That had certainly been his game plan, before the injury. Unfortunately, life was what happened while you were making other plans.

Ah, well, running a supermarket was hard work, but he made a good living at it. He could afford to send Boyd and Brenda to any college or university they chose.

A sharp pain stabbed his knee. He frowned and checked his watch, saw that less than two hours had passed since he'd popped four aspirin tablets, and decided he'd better wait a while.

Maybe he'd get caught up in reading and forget the pain. He glanced at both book jackets again and chose the courtroom drama, written by a best-selling author. He scooted his easy chair closer to the fireplace, propped his feet on an ottoman and opened the book.

Fifteen minutes later, he laid the book aside. Even though the author was one of his favorites, he couldn't get into the story. And he still wasn't sleepy. His knee hurt, but more persistent was the nagging worry that had settled at the back of his mind when Lily told him that Sherwood Draper was coming to Victoria Springs to direct the church's Christmas pageant. He knew his wife was behind it, but he'd known better than to confront her. She'd have denied it and accused him of not trusting her. So he'd kept quiet, stewing in silence.

Lily was going to spend hours and hours for the next couple of weeks in the company of that pompous, self-important ass. Denny had pegged Draper for a fake within thirty minutes after meeting him in Vail. The man thought he was Laurence Olivier. Talked endlessly about his "stage career." It never seemed to occur to him that he was a flat-out failure, reduced to teaching at some dinky junior college.

It would have been laughable if Lily hadn't fallen for the man's line. Of course, Lily had had a wandering eye for a while now. Five years ago, when she hit thirty-five, she had begun to talk about having some fun while she was still young enough to enjoy it. She'd proceeded to indulge in several flirtations, all in good fun, she assured him. "Everybody knows I don't mean anything by it," she'd say. And, actually, he didn't think the flirtations had gone beyond that.

You couldn't order Lily around, so he'd tried to humor her. After all, he might be past his prime and feeling worn down by life, but until a few months ago, Lily had still been in her thirties. He was determined to be a good sport. He'd told her she could redecorate the house, get some new furniture. He'd actually let her talk him into a family ski trip, even though he wasn't about to risk getting on skis for the first time in his life and injuring his knee again.

They'd met the Drapers at the ski lodge. Not surprisingly, he'd been bored stiff while the twins and Lily— particularly Lily—had had a blast. The Vail trip had merely whetted Lily's appetite for travel. As soon as school was out, they'd sent the twins to her parents' and spent a month in the British Isles. Lily had said she knew she'd never get him over there again, so she wanted to see *everything*. Denny was pretty sure they had, too. By the end of the first week, he'd wanted desperately to come back to Victoria Springs. When they finally did return a month later, he'd never been so glad to see home in his life. If he never set eyes on another crumbling castle or stepped on another airplane, it would be too soon.

Next on Lily's fun agenda for them was bridge lessons.

At Lily's insistence, they'd joined a country club, too. But golfing and tennis made Denny's knee hurt, and he told Lily he didn't want to be seen in a bathing suit until he'd lost some weight. She'd glared at him and snapped, "Right, like that's going to happen."

Lately, Lily was often out of patience with him, and he lived with the fear that some day, one of Lily's infatuations would become a full-blown affair and she'd leave him.

Gazing into the fireplace, he closed his big hands into fists. Well, that would be a cold day in hell. His wife exhausted him, but he wasn't going to let her go. For sure, he wasn't going to sit back and watch some mealy-mouthed junior college teacher, who did well to pull down thirty thousand a year, steal his wife. His glance strayed to the gun cabinet where the hunting rifles he hadn't used in years were locked up. He'd blow that pompous pissant Draper to pieces if he touched Lily.

Then the thought of Lily trying to live on thirty thou a year made him smile, and he relaxed his clenched fingers. Surely his free-spending wife had better sense than to go that far. Still, he probably should find a couple of hours tomorrow to drop in at the church, let Draper—and Lily— know he might appear unannounced at any time. Lily was always going on about his not wanting to get involved in community affairs. Maybe he'd make himself useful with the pageant, if it didn't take too much of his time away from the store. Unlike most of the businesses in Victoria Springs, the supermarket did a brisk trade during December.

He pushed himself out of the easy chair and went to the kitchen. The leather soles of his house slippers made loud slapping sounds on the Mexican tile. Like most of the other rooms in the house, the big country kitchen was done up gaily for Christmas. A centerpiece of holly, red balls, and fat red candles sat in the center of the kitchen table on a runner decorated with reindeer and jolly, red-cheeked Santas. Christmas wreaths and a small red-and-green quilt adorned the walls.

"Joy to the world," he muttered dryly.

Denny poured himself a glass of wine, hoping it would make him sleepy. Wine usually affected him that way, though it might take two glasses.

He glanced out a kitchen window and saw a few flakes of snow in the light from the yard lamp. If the snow was as heavy as the TV weather man predicted, traffic at the store would be way down tomorrow. It would give him an excuse to drive Lily to the church. Even better, a deep snowfall might cause the pastor to cancel pageant practice and keep Lily at home.

Standing at the counter, sipping the wine, he saw a movement from the corner of his eye. A cockroach skittered across the tile floor. Denny let out a yelp of outrage, set the wine glass down, ran across the room, and slammed his house slipper down on the cockroach before it disappeared beneath the baseboard. Lily hated bugs, and even though they rarely had a problem, she had the whole place treated every year. Denny couldn't remember when he had last seen a roach in the house. This one had probably arrived in a grocery bag. He fought them constantly at the supermarket. Roaches were always a problem where there was so much food around.

He hoped he hadn't awakened Lily or the kids, yelping like that. He listened for sounds from the bedrooms, but heard nothing. Everybody but Denny was snug in their beds. With visions of sugar plums dancing in their heads—or, in Lily's case, visions of . . .

He brushed that thought aside.

He tore off a section of paper towel and cleaned his house slipper. Then he tore off another section and picked up the squashed roach. Carrying it to the kitchen waste basket, he gazed without expression at the squishy, yellow and black remains of the bug.

He wished he could eliminate Sherwood Draper as easily.

# Chapter 3

For once the weather man got it exactly right. A deep covering of pristine white surrounded Iris House when Tess awoke the next morning, and snow still fell. Tess burrowed beneath the covers, with only her face and the top of her head exposed, and gazed through her bedroom window at the big flakes drifting down. Overnight the backyard had been transformed into a hushed, pure, alien place. It was a perfect day to stay inside in front of a roaring fire—sip hot chocolate, roast a few marshmallows, cook up a big pot of chili for dinner. Alas, it was not to be.

"Get up, Tess," she told herself.

Maybe Pastor Matt would call off the pageant practice today. Blanche would know. She'd call her as soon as she was sure the Tandys were up. In the meantime . . .

Oh, blast, she had the Drapers upstairs. Could Gertie get to Iris House through the snow? If not, Tess would have to make breakfast for her guests. She groaned aloud at the very idea. She was no match for Gertie in the kitchen.

She'd better make sure she had the ingredients on hand for an emergency breakfast. She thought there were some of Gertie's home-made muffins in the freezer, and perhaps a bacon-and-carrot quiche. With sausage links and fruit, it would do.

Bracing herself, Tess crawled from beneath the warm covers. Shivering, she grabbed her robe and stepped into the hall to turn up the furnace thermostat.

Back in her bedroom, she dressed quickly in a bulky rust-colored sweater, chocolate-brown wool pants, and sturdy boots. After running a brush through her curly auburn hair and applying a few dashes of makeup, she hurried down the hall, pausing outside the bedroom where Madison slept. Touching the doorknob, she hesitated, then dropped her hand. If Madison's mood hadn't improved, it was going to be an uncomfortable day for both of them. Tess decided to let Madison sleep as long as possible.

In her kitchen, which was a smaller replica of the main Iris House kitchen, she fed an insistent Primrose, then left the apartment and crossed the mahogany-colored glazed tile floor of the foyer. Light falling through the irises in the stained glass panels on either side of the front door threw warm yellow, red, and purple splotches on the tile.

Entering the big guest parlor with its chintz and velvet Victorian furnishings, she heard a murmur of voices coming from the kitchen at the back of the house.

As Tess crossed the parlor, she heard Gertie say, "Land sakes, imagine you two kids coming all the way from Paris, France alone. The very thought of flying over the ocean scares me spitless. Don't know why it seems worse than flying over land. Weren't you even a little bit frightened?"

Tess passed beneath the archway that separated the parlor from the dining room. The massive, oval dining table was already set with navy place mats and the china specially made for Iris House, which was decorated with hand-painted irises the color of ripe raspberries. A raspberry-colored napkin was rolled in a silver napkin ring beside each plate.

Gertie had started a fire in the dining room fireplace where flames curled lazily around hickory logs. Tess had found raspberry-colored Christmas balls and candles and arranged them with lots of holly on the dining room's dark, carved mantlepiece. It was the only Christmas decorating she'd done so far and she needed to shop for decorations for the other rooms in the house. She wanted it to be perfect for Christmas. Iris House would be closed to guests from the twenty-second until after the New Year. Gertie and Nedra, Tess's housekeeper, would take a holiday. As for Tess, she was hosting Christmas dinner for the whole Darcy clan. Fortunately, Aunt Dahlia and Zelda would be on hand to help her.

As Tess approached the kitchen doorway, Curt was revealed, leaning on the center island, a big mug of hot chocolate and an empty plate in front of him. He popped the last bite of a fresh cinnamon roll into his mouth and said, "Naw, we fly all the time." He was a skinny, long-legged thirteen-year-old, with light brown eyes and freckles on his nose. When he'd walked off the plane yesterday, Tess had been surprised to see that he'd grown several inches since last year; he was an inch taller than she now and would probably top his father's six feet before he was through growing.

Curt had worn a sport jacket and tie for the journey from France, undoubtedly at his mother's insistence. This morning he'd chosen his own wardrobe, jeans and a quilted, dingy-white pullover that looked like insulated underwear that had been washed with a load of dark clothes. He hadn't bothered combing his short, brown hair, which stood up in tufts.

Tess's worry over breakfast dissipated at the sight of Gertie drizzling thin sugar frosting over a second pan of cinnamon rolls fresh from the oven. A pitcher of fresh-squeezed orange juice sat on the pickled-pine breakfront near the stove next to bowls of fresh eggs, egg substitute for the cholesterol conscious, chopped ham, chopped onions, mushrooms, pimento, and grated cheese—swiss and cheddar.

"Good morning," Tess greeted them. "Couldn't wait for breakfast, huh, Curt?"

He grinned at her. "You call this breakfast?"

"Just a little appetizer for a growing boy." Gertie, who'd raised two boys of her own, gazed at Curt fondly.

"Sleep well?" Tess asked Curt.

"I died." His brown eyes sparkled. "Did you see the snow?"

"It's kind of hard to miss," Tess said.

"I remember from last year that you've got some humongous hills in this town."

"That's true." In fact, Iris House was one of the first big Victorian homes built atop what had passed for Victoria Spring's nob hill in the early days of the town's existence.

"Don't guess you have a sled," he said hopefully.

"No, sorry. Maybe we can get downtown this afternoon and buy one. We need to get a Christmas tree, too, before they're all picked over. Depends on how bad the streets are, though. Gertie, I hope you didn't risk your life to get here."

"I've got chains," Gertie said. "Not much traffic this early, and I took it slow." She turned from the cinnamon rolls and planted her hands on her wide hips. Instead of one of her many comfortable tent-dresses, she was wearing a purple-and-yellow plaid flannel shirt, baggy pants, and heavy white socks with stretchy pink house slippers. A pair of thick-soled work boots which probably belonged to Gertie's husband sat in a puddle of melted snow on the mat near the back door. Her sandy hair was held back with a wide red headband which had also served to keep her ears warm on the drive over. "I hope *you're* not planning on going out."

"I have to go to the church, but Luke's taking me in Sidney's Jeep. Unless the pageant practice is called off. I'll check with Blanche Tandy a little later."

"I called Nedra a few minutes ago," Gertie said. "She can't get her car out of her driveway."

"Thank goodness there's only the suite to clean." Tess glanced at Curt. "You'll have to pick up after yourself for a day or two, 'till our housekeeper can come in."

Curt shrugged good-naturedly. "So what else is new? I have to do it all the time at home."

"Poor, mistreated child," Tess teased.

"Tell Mom that, will ya?"

"I can change the sheets and bath linens in the Darcy Flame suite after breakfast," Gertie offered.

"Thank you, Gertie. I'll take care of everything else."

"Will there be any kids at the pageant practice?" Curt asked.

"Maybe," Tess said. "School will probably be cancelled because of the snow, and there are a few teenagers in the choir."

"Can I go with you?"

"If you want to." Good, that took care of what to do with Curt today. But what about Madison? "I warn you, though, somebody is apt to put you to work."

He shrugged again. "That's okay. Might be kind of fun." Curt had always been an even-tempered, cooperative child, and hitting his teen years hadn't changed him. Tess was extremely fond of her young half-brother. Suddenly, Curt added impulsively, "I'm glad we got to come to Victoria Springs early, Tess."

Tess smiled and smoothed down his hair. "You know what, I'm glad, too. I don't think Madison's very happy to be here, though."

He expelled a grunt of disgust. "Madison's a real pain in the as—er, butt sometimes. She's just mad 'cause she's missing a couple of parties her friends are having. She's afraid Dan, that's her boyfriend, will take up with some other girl while she's gone."

"Oh?"

"Yeah, not that it would be this great catastrophe, if you ask me. Dan's a real jerk, thinks he'd God's gift to the female race and big stuff 'cause his dad's some high-ranking army officer. Mom says Madison is too young to have real dates, anyway, so she only gets together with Dan at school and parties. Mom always calls ahead to make sure the parties will be chaperoned. Madison hates that.''

"Fourteen can be a difficult age for a girl," Tess said noncommitally. Then, hearing steps on the stairs, she glanced toward the kitchen doorway. "Sounds like the Drapers are coming down.''

"I'll get started on the omelets," Gertie said. "Curt, what do you want in yours?''

Curt didn't even have to think about it. "Onions, ham, and lots of cheddar cheese.''

"Curt," Tess said, "would you mind waking Madison? Tell her if she wants a hot breakfast, she should get dressed and come to the dining room right away.''

Curt grimaced. "I'll need a suit of armor. She'll throw whatever she can get her hands on.''

Tess chuckled and shook her head. "Sorry, we're fresh out of chain mail.''

Curt sighed. "Okay, I'll wake her up. I'm used to being abused.''

"You're breaking my heart," Tess said, patting his cheek. "Seriously, I need to know if she wants to go to the church with us. If she stays here, she'll be alone in the house when Gertie goes home. There are plenty of books in the library, if she'd rather read.''

"Madison? Read something that's not assigned by a teacher? I don't think so.''

"Well, there's always TV, but there's not much on during the day. Anyway, she needs to decide. Here or the church.''

He rolled his eyes and headed for the door. "She's gonna love those choices.''

Blanche Tandy hung up the phone and returned to her chair at the kitchen table, where her husband, Mike, was finishing off a stack of pancakes and keeping an eye on the small TV set on the kitchen counter. The names of schools that would be closed today scrolled down the screen.

"Pastor Matt refuses to call off pageant practice," Blanche said gloomily.

Mike, still watching the TV screen, said, "There's Victoria Springs. No school today. Eddie will be happy about that."

Eddie Zoller had been living with the Tandys for five months now. Eddie's mother had died when he was thirteen, and he'd pretty much looked after himself after that, until he moved in with Blanche and Mike. He'd been working part-time at the store for the past year, and he was quite dedicated. But he'd gotten in with a rough crowd at school and early last summer he and his friends had vandalized a couple of business buildings. Eddie's father, who drank and disappeared for long periods of time, hadn't shown up for the hearing, but Mike and Blanche had. Mike had been allowed to put in a good word for Eddie and the judge gave Eddie a year's probation, then ordered the boy into foster care.

Throughout the hearing, Eddie had looked at his knees, his long, lank hair falling over his face. Blanche thought Eddie hid behind that hair because he was too embarrassed by his father to look people in the eye. She wasn't even sure he was listening to the proceedings until the judge said "foster care." Then Eddie's head shot up and he'd glanced at Mike and Blanche with panic in his eyes.

It was a clear plea for help. Blanche, who'd always had a soft spot for Eddie, had talked Mike into letting him move in with them. She was convinced that all the boy needed was some structure and discipline and people who cared about him. Mike had been less sure, but Blanche had been right.

Nobody had said a word about his hair, though Blanche had had to bite her tongue many times. It wasn't the length of his hair that she minded, but the fact that it was always in his face drove her crazy. She wanted to suggest a pony tail, at least, but she exercised admirable restraint and kept still. Then one day, a couple of months after he'd moved in, Eddie had come home with a short, neat haircut.

He'd changed in other ways, as well. He could talk to adults without ducking his head now. At first, he would hardly say two words at a time to Blanche, but now he could be absolutely loquacious. He'd been failing half his classes when he came to live with them and now he had all B's and C's.

Gradually, he'd distanced himself from his former friends and had become involved in the youth group at church. He even sang in the choir with Mike, whom he clearly idolized. It was an amazing transformation. People at church often remarked on how much Eddie had changed since he moved in with the Tandys.

Mike turned off the TV and rubbed his stomach with a satisfied sigh. He was a burly bear of a man, his brown eyes set wide beneath thick brows. The last couple of years, a few silver hairs had appeared in his heavy beard and moustache.

"So Pastor Matt insists on having pageant practice today," he remarked

Blanche cradled her coffee cup in both hands. "Yes. He said he'll pick up the new guy in his truck, if necessary, and he can work with whoever makes it to the church. We're getting a late start this year, anyway, because of bringing in an outsider to direct."

Mike stared at her, his mouth half-open. "Whoa. Did I miss something? What outsider? What're you talking about?"

Sometimes she got carried away talking, and forgot to fill in important details. "Oh, I guess I didn't tell you. Pastor Matt has hired a drama teacher from Colorado to direct the pageant this year."

"Does Claire Chandler know about this?"

"She should by now. The pastor asked Tess Darcy to give her the message."

Mike lifted an eyebrow. "Cowardly of the rev."

Blanche gave him a faint smile. "That's what I thought, but I'm glad I wasn't the one who had to tell Claire. Everybody else will find out today at practice. I really should be there. If Claire starts something, somebody has to stop her. Do you have to go to the hardware store today?"

"Not till after noon, if then. I called and Beasley made it in. Business ought to be slow today; he can handle it by himself. I need to talk to this new man about the choir selections for the pageant." For the past few months, since the choir director moved away, Mike had taken over those duties. It was supposed to be temporary—Mike had a good ear, if no formal music training—but so far nobody else had shown an interest in the job.

Blanche finished her coffee and went to stand at the kitchen window, looking out.

"It's only two blocks to the church," Mike said. "We can walk if we have to."

She watched two bundled-up neighbor children who were building a snowman in the yard next door. "I'd enjoy walking," she said. "It's so beautiful out there." Abruptly the children abandoned the half-finished snowman, as the boy chased the girl around the house, pelting her with snowballs.

Mike came up behind Blanche and put his arms around her. He rubbed his beard against her cheek, a gesture that she found comforting. "Hey, you worried about Claire?"

She sighed. "I think it's silly of the pastor to bring in a stranger for the pageant, besides being unnecessary. I guess we can thank Lily Brookside. It was her idea. When Lily gets a bee in her bonnet, she won't take no for an answer."

"Lily, huh?" muttered Mike. "Well, that'll tick Claire off real good. My advice, let Pastor Matt deal with it."

"Oh, sure. I'll bet he hides in his office all day. He'll come out only when he knows the storm has passed." Pastor Matt was a big hit with the younger crowd, especially the teenagers, and Blanche liked him well enough, but he had a way of being busy elsewhere when a fuss was brewing at church.

Blanche laughed suddenly. "Oh, look at those kids, Mike. They're making snow angels. I wish . . ." She didn't finish, but they both knew what she wished.

He kissed her cheek as his arms tightened around her. "You've done a great job with Eddie."

She nodded, accepting the compliment. "He's basically a good kid, but after another year of high school, he'll be out and on his own." She loved Eddie, she really did, but he was practically grown when he came to them. Blanche still ached to hold a baby in her arms.

"You're all I need, honey bunch," Mike murmured against her cheek.

She didn't look at him. "Honestly?"

"Cross my heart."

She believed him. Ten years ago they'd lost a baby girl when she was just a few days old. Mike would have loved her, if she'd survived, but he had never really felt the deep longing for a baby that she lived with. Following the loss of their daughter, Blanche had suffered three miscarriages. Finally, she had accepted that she would probably never have another baby and she'd wanted to adopt.

In one of the rare instances in her marriage, Mike had refused to cooperate. If they hadn't lost their little girl, he'd have done his darndest to be a good father but, he finally admitted, he was afraid he would've fallen far short. Maybe God was trying to tell them they shouldn't have children—no, he didn't want to adopt. They still had each other, and that's all they needed.

For a while, she had resented his attitude. With time, her resentment had faded because she thought she understood why he felt as he did. Mike had no family. He'd never had brothers or sisters and he'd lost his parents before Blanche met him. Though he would never talk about it, Blanche suspected that his childhood had been extremely unhappy. She didn't believe he'd been physically abused—she'd always heard that abused children became abusers themselves, and Mike had never even raised his voice to her or to Eddie. Though he hadn't really wanted to take on a troubled sixteen-year-old at first, she'd dug in her heels and he'd finally given in. And he was good with the boy, he really was. As for Eddie, his main goal in life seemed to be to earn Mike's approval.

Blanche had hoped having Eddie around might cause Mike to change his mind about adopting. They might be too old now to get a baby through an agency, but she'd wanted to talk to their doctor about a private adoption. But Mike hadn't changed his mind, and she'd finally accepted it. No point in getting resentful all over again, when Mike was such a good husband in every other way.

She'd given it a lot of thought and had come to the conclusion that Mike didn't miss having a close, loving family because he'd never known one. Even though he hadn't been physically abused, Blanche thought he had been unwanted and neglected as a child, that his parents had been cold and unloving. Though such people were beyond Blanche's understanding, Mike's parents had probably looked upon him as an unasked-for nuisance. Mike had told her once that when he left Iowa, he never wanted to go back. Oblique though it was, that was one of the few comments he'd ever made about his childhood.

Fortunately, Mike seemed to enjoy their annual visits to her parents in Florida, and he couldn't be more hospitable when they or Blanche's sister and her family visited Victoria Springs. Yet those visits never seemed to spark any interest in seeing his own remaining relatives— indeed, Blanche wasn't even sure he *had* any relatives still living. He'd told her once, early in their marriage, that he had a couple of cousins back in Iowa, but he'd never been close to them and had no desire to renew acquaintances.

It was as if, when he married her, Mike had taken Blanche's family as his own. Those of her friends who didn't get along with their in-laws told her she didn't know how lucky she was.

The telephone rang and she shook off her introspection.

Mike answered and told the caller that, yes, pageant practice was on. "Tess Darcy," he said to Blanche when he'd hung up. "Sounded like she was hoping Pastor Matt would call it off."

"Don't we all," Blanche said. "You'd better go wake up Eddie. Tell him I'm cooking his pancakes. What do you think about shopping for a Christmas tree later today? I noticed some really nice ones in that lot next to Denny's supermarket."

He lifted an eyebrow. "So early? We never do that before the fifteenth."

"We have Eddie now," Blanche said. "I don't think he has many happy memories of Christmas, and I want this one to be special for him. He'll get a kick out of decorating the tree."

"Yeah, and you'll get a bigger kick out of watching him."

She gave him a sideways look and he smiled. "That's true," she said. She added briskly, "Go wake Eddie and I'll fix his breakfast. We need to get to the church."

Mike released her. "Yeah, wouldn't want Claire to get there ahead of us."

## Chapter 4

After calling the Tandys' house from the phone in
her apartment, Tess returned to the dining room
where her guests were having breakfast. While she
made her phone call and ate the cinnamon roll she'd
taken with her, Madison, in jeans and a canary-
yellow sweater, had joined Curt and the Drapers at
the table.

Tess greeted the Drapers, then added, "Good
morning, Madison."

Still puffy-eyed from sleep, Madison raked shiny,
falling hair from her eyes and managed a small
smile. " 'Morning, Tess," she murmured. Madison
had her mother's dark hair and gray eyes, and like
Tess's Aunt Dahlia, she'd gotten the best of the
Darcy facial features—high cheekbones, a small,
straight nose, a wide mouth, and perfect teeth. Madison was a budding beauty. Like her Aunt Dahlia
before her, Madison would break some hearts before she settled down.

At least, Tess reflected, unlike Dahlia, Madison
didn't have a plain, older sister like Iris who would
have to watch boys coming and going and hear the
telephone's constant ringing, knowing that none of
the calls was for her. Poor Iris, she thought, remembering with fondness her late aunt who had left her

the Darcy family home which Tess had turned into the bed and breakfast.

Morning light, reflecting off the snow, brightened the dining room, with its dark, heavy furniture, and the crackling fire added a cozy touch. Framed in the wide window, white-laced shrubs grew next to the fence, where snow was mounded along the wrought-iron top like sugar frosting. Beyond the fence and a wide expanse of pristine white was a snow-roofed, yellow Victorian house, surrounded by its own white-mounded shrubs. The scene could have been taken straight from a Currier and Ives print.

Sherwood Draper, who'd come to breakfast in a hunter-green corduroy jacket with elbow patches and, of all things, a silk ascot, tossed his head to sweep back the wave of black hair which fell carelessly across his brow. Throwing his hair back that way seemed to be a habitual gesture, and Tess suspected Draper believed it gave him a sophisticated air. He probably thought the same thing about the pipe he often fondled or held between his teeth. Last night, when Tess told him that Iris House was a smoke-free environment, he'd assured her that he never actually *smoked* the pipe.

With one finger, Draper casually stroked a silver-dusted sideburn that grew halfway down his long cheek. While trying to appear nonchalant, he was taking careful note of Madison, repeatedly glancing sideways at the girl to study her profile between bites of breakfast.

Madison didn't appear to notice. She was probably still too sleepy to be aware of Draper's regard. Or perhaps she was used to being stared at by men old enough to be her father.

Tess poured a cup of coffee from the silver pot on the sideboard and pulled out a Windsor chair. "I just talked to the church choir director. There will be a pageant practice at ten, for whoever shows up. The minister will pick you up about nine-fifteen, Professor Draper."

"Splendid," Draper said. His eyelids at half-mast, he

smiled at Madison when she finally glanced up at him.
"There's much work to do in a very short time." He
waved long, elegant fingers at Tess. "And please, my
dear, call me Sherwood."

Tess nodded, but she doubted she could do that. There
was something too lofty in Sherwood Draper's attitude
for her ever to be comfortable addressing him by his given
name, as she did most of her guests.

Mavis, who was looking particularly attractive this
morning in a rose-colored sweater, stared sourly through
plastic-framed eyeglasses into her coffee cup. The frames
had flakes embedded in them that made them sparkle
when they caught the light. Mavis had remained silent
since Tess returned to the dining room, but now she grum-
bled, "Personally, I think it's asinine to expect people to
get out on a day like this."

"It's a glorious day," her husband exclaimed. He
swept one magnanimous hand toward the window, as
though he himself were responsible for the beauty of the
scene. "Look at that. It's like a Christmas card."

Mavis, who sat with her back to the window, didn't
turn around.

"More to the point," Draper said, eyeing his wife
shrewdly, "time is of the essence. Mavis, my dear, you
don't have to go, you know. Why don't you stay here
where you'll be warm and cozy."

"If you'd rather stay," Tess put in, "there's a well-
stocked library on the third floor. And there's soup and
sandwich fixings for lunch, if you don't mind helping
yourself."

"Thank you, but I'll go along and help with the pageant," Mavis said, forcing a smile as she met her husband's gaze. "I'm sure they'll need all the help they can
get."

Tess looked at Madison, who was picking at her omelet. "What about you, Madison, are you staying in? Or
would you rather go to the church with Curt and me?"

Madison put down her fork, cradled her chin in her

hand, and turned droopy gray eyes on Tess. "Would I be here alone?"

"After Gertie leaves, yes."

Madison glanced at Curt, who was polishing off a three-egg omelet and another cinnamon roll. "Curtie," she said sweetly, "why don't you stay here with me?"

He looked at Tess and rolled his eyes. "Don't call me Curtie. And I already promised Tess I'd go and help."

"*C'est ennuyeux,*" Madison muttered.

"Not as boring as staying here and listening to you moan and groan about Danny boy," Curt told her.

"Fine," Madison snapped. "Don't do me any favors."

"There might be other kids at the church," Curt said, ignoring her burst of temper. "And, after practice, Tess says we can get a sled."

"Ooo," Madison crooned, her eyes wide with mock excitement. "*C'est vraiment incroyable.*"

Tess had forgotten most of her college French, but she thought she recognized the word "incredible," and she certainly picked up on the tone of heavy sarcasm.

Sherwood Draper cleared his throat. "My dear Madison. May I ask how long you plan to be visiting your sister?"

Madison gave him a startled look as though he'd just that moment materialized at the table, like a ghost. "Till after the new year. My parents will be here later and we'll return to France together."

He beamed at her. "Wonderful."

She raked her hair out of her eyes and muttered crossly, "Not really." Draper continued to study her. "Why are you looking at me like that?"

"Forgive me," Draper apologized, "I don't mean to stare, my dear, but there's something about you that seems so—familiar."

What is this? Tess wondered. A variation on the old haven't-we-met-somewhere-before routine? As a teacher, Sherwood Draper was surely wise enough to avoid any hint of flirtation with underage girls, but Tess decided she would keep an eye on him, anyway.

"It will come to me eventually," Draper said. "My dear Madison, has anyone ever told you what a perfectly lovely face you have? Such fabulous bones!"

Madison's cross expression faded and she blushed prettily. Suddenly she didn't look at all out of sorts. "*Merci.*"

"And what a flawless complexion!" Draper exclaimed. He touched the tips of his fingers to his mouth and made a kiss-throwing motion in Madison's direction. "Like a dew-kissed rose."

Curt darted a look at Tess and stuck his finger in his mouth, pretending to gag. Tess agreed with him, though she frowned to discourage Curt.

"Madison," Draper went on, "you would be perfect for the part of the Virgin Mary in the pageant. Scholars believe she was quite young, probably about your age." He closed his eyes and continued dreamily, "I'm considering borrowing some ideas from a unique performance of *Hamlet* in which I performed several times during my stage career in London. Burton played Hamlet, but the director told me in private, after he saw me act, that he wished he'd cast me in the role." He opened his eyes and leaned both elbows on the table. Speaking to Madison, he continued, "Much of the drama that is taking shape in my mind would be in pantomime. A series of dramatic vignettes which would put a modern twist on the old Christmas story. You'd have to learn only a few lines. Mostly, you'd stand there and look modest and innocently stunning and communicate with those large, expressive gray eyes."

Curt covered his mouth with his hand to hide a grin. Tess could hardly blame him. Honestly, Sherwood Draper was spreading it on like soft butter with a putty knife. The man was so pompous and pleased with himself that Tess had to hold back a peal of laughter.

Such lavish flattery wouldn't make Madison any easier to live with, either. Furthermore, Tess wasn't sure how the traditionalists among the congregation would like Draper's "modern twist" on the Christmas story.

Madison basked in Draper's attention. She sat straighter in her chair. "Actually, I'm thinking of becoming an actress. My teachers say I have talent in the dramatic arts."

"Do you now?"

"*Oui*. I played Juliet in the school play last year."

"I'm sure you were perfect!" Draper exclaimed.

Madison lowered her eyes modestly. "I got a standing ovation."

Curt exchanged another disgusted look with Tess and held up two fingers. "Posers," he mouthed.

Tess gave a quick shake of her head, but Draper and Madison were too engrossed in their conversation to notice him. As for Mavis Draper, she had been watching the exchange between her husband and Madison with troubled interest and deeply etched frown lines between her eyebrows.

"You must say yes, Madison! Please honor me by taking the part of Mary?"

"If you really want me to," Madison said demurely.

"Perfect type-casting!" Draper exclaimed.

"At least," responded Madison, "it will be something to do while I'm here."

Draper clapped his hands delightedly. "Splendid." He pushed back his chair and, with a big smile for Madison which managed to exclude everybody else, said, "I'll see you at the church then." She might as well have been the only other person at the table.

Looking flustered, Mavis got up hastily and followed her husband from the dining room.

"What a prize jerk," Curt grunted. "And what's that thing around his neck?"

"An ascot, you bumpkin," Madison retorted. "Don't you know anything?"

"I know a butthead when I see one!" He fluttered his fingers and added in a falsetto tone, "Oh, dear me, I was in Hamlet when I was on the stage in London. I hate to brag, but I was better than Burton.''

Madison groaned. "*Merde*! You're too dense to understand the artistic temperament.''

"Oh, pul-leeze!''

"Okay, kids," Tess said, getting up, "let's get a move on. Why don't the two of you help Gertie clear the table, then get ready to go to the church. I need to make a couple of phone calls, and spruce up the suite as soon as the Drapers leave. Luke will be here to pick us up at ten.''

The steepled church sat atop a gentle hill, its white walls surrounded by snow-draped trees and shrubs. Stained-glass windows depicting angels and Old Testament characters sparkled with deep green and wine and gold, in sharp contrast to the whiteness all around. Another Currier and Ives print, Tess thought, as she climbed out of the Jeep. The cobbled walk had been shoveled. Already footprints sank deep into the surrounding snow.

The Tandys and Eddie tromped toward the walk, followed by the Brookside family. Mike called a greeting and Tess waved.

Luke got out of the driver's side and joined Tess beside the Jeep. "I'm surprised to see Denny here.''

"He probably didn't want Lily or the twins driving," Tess said, "but I can't see him hanging around long.''

Glancing past the Brooksides, she scanned the parking lot. Her Aunt Dahlia's Cadillac was there, which surprised her until she saw the chains on its tires. She didn't see Claire Chandler's car. If we're lucky, she told herself, Claire will stay at home. As unlikely as that was.

Curt and Madison tumbled from the Cherokee's back seat. Luke had brought some rubber boots for Curt to wear over his shoes and Tess had found an old pair of boots in her closet for Madison. They were a size too big, but an improvement over the thin-soled loafers Madison had been prepared to wear to the church.

Madison stood beside the jeep, balancing herself with

a gloved hand on the hood, and stared toward the church. "Who's *that*, Tess?"

Tess watched the Tandys and the Brooksides approaching the front door of the church. "Who?"

"That boy."

"Which one?"

"The cute one in the red jacket."

The Tandys disappeared into the church as the Brooksides reached the door and Denny caught it before it swung shut.

"That's Boyd Brookside," Tess said.

"Oh, Boy-eed," Curt stage-whispered, "Madison thinks you're awful cute."

"Shut up, dumbhead," Madison murmured, but the words held no fire. Her attention was still fixed on the heavy front doors of the church where Boyd, the last of the Brooksides to enter, hesitated with his hand gripping the door handle. He pulled off his cap, revealing tousled dark hair, and glanced over his shoulder, straight at Madison. "Hi, Tess. Hi, Luke." Boyd looked at Madison as he spoke. Then he grinned, stuffed his cap into his jacket pocket, pulled open the door, and stepped inside.

A little frown creased Madison's smooth brow. "Who's that girl with him?"

"His twin sister, Brenda," Tess said.

Madison's expression cleared. "Oh. How old are they?"

"Seventeen," Tess told her. "They're seniors at the high school."

"He's too old for you, Mad," Curt teased.

"That is *so* not true," she retorted. "I've always been mature for my age."

Curt snorted. "Yeah, I've really noticed that." He bent and picked up a handful of snow. "Better watch it, sis. I may have to report to Danny boy that you're flirting with another guy."

"You'll do no such thing, you little cretin! And I'm not flirting. I haven't even spoken to him yet."

"Only 'cause you haven't had the chance. How much is it worth for me to keep my mouth shut with Danny?"

"I don't have to pay you," Madison retorted. "I'll just kill you if you open your big mouth."

"You and what army?" Chortling like a villain in a melodrama, Curt patted the ball of snow in his hand.

"Oh, no!" Madison shrieked and ran toward the church. Suddenly, she was a kid again instead of a young woman trying to sound sophisticated by spouting French.

Curt's snowball exploded against the back of Madison's coat. "I'll get you for that!" she yelled.

"Like I said, you and what army!"

She crossed her eyes and stuck out her tongue at him just before the door closed behind her.

"Hey, wait up!" Curt brushed the snow off his gloves and ran to catch his sister.

Tess took Luke's arm as they approached the church at a more sedate pace.

"Who's Danny?" Luke inquired.

"A boy back in Paris," Tess said. "He goes to school with Curt and Madison. According to Curt he's the son of a high-ranking army officer and thinks he's God's gift."

"Sounds perfect for Madison."

Tess nodded, laughing. "She's not allowed to date."

"I should hope not. She's what, fourteen?"

"Yes, and according to Curt, she only sees this Danny at school and parties. Coming to Victoria Springs early caused her to miss two of her friends' get-togethers."

"A teenage catastrophe," Luke observed.

"Madison moped all the way home from the airport. I wanted to turn her over my knee."

"Might do her a world of good."

"It would throw her into shock. I'm sure she's never had a spanking in her life. Dad doesn't believe in it. He takes you into his study and has a little talk."

"It worked with you, sweetheart. Don't know how well

it's working with Madison, but she sure seems in good spirits now.''

"It didn't hurt that Sherwood Draper told her how pretty she is and asked her to play Mary in the drama.''

"I thought we already had people to play the main parts. Somebody's liable to have her feelings hurt.''

"As I recall, we didn't have anybody for Mary. But, frankly, I don't think Draper will lose any sleep over it if he has to boot somebody out of the part. He's very—well, sure of himself. And Madison was thrilled to be asked to be in the drama.''

"She seems to have forgotten Danny boy, too,'' Luke added with a grin. "Out of sight, out of mind, right?''

"Looks like,'' Tess agreed.

He bent suddenly and scooped up a handful of snow.

"Don't you dare!'' Tess yelped and started to run. Her boots slid from beneath her and Luke's snowball whizzed over her head as she landed, laughing, on her backside in the snow. She scooped snow in both gloved hands and scrambled to her feet. Luke was bending over for more snow, his rear end providing a target too tempting to resist. She hurled the snowball and hit the target.

He yelped and whirled around. "Payback time!''

Tess held up both hands. "We're even, okay?''

He patted the handful of snow into a ball. "What do you mean even? I missed you.''

She brushed the seat of her slacks and began walking toward the church as fast as she dared. "Can I help it if I'm a better marksman than you?''

"Oh yeah?''

She reached the church without another fall, while managing to duck his snowball. "See what I mean? You just don't have the eye for it.''

Luke shook his head. "Conceit is an unattractive thing in a woman. Next time,'' he muttered, striding after her. As they stomped snow off their boots on the stone porch, the Chandlers' Oldsmobile crept around the corner and turned into the church parking lot.

"Uh-oh," Luke said. "Claire's here."

"Bill's with her," Tess said. "Good. He's such a sensible, collected man."

Luke looked down at her as he reached for the door handle. "You think he'll make Claire behave?"

"I can hope."

"But don't lay any bets on it."

## *Chapter 5*

Tess stepped quietly into the dim foyer. There was barely enough light for her to recognize Blanche Tandy, who stood at the door leading into the sanctuary, and Mike, who was hanging his overcoat on a hook beside three others. Blanche peered through a narrow pane in the sanctuary door and said, "That must be him."

"Who?" Mike asked, coming up behind her.

"Sherwood Draper—the pageant director. The pastor is introducing him now."

Mike, the hood of his sweatshirt still pulled up, craned his neck to look over her shoulder. For a few moments, the two of them stood there in silence. Then Mike muttered, "The man's wearing an ascot. An ascot, for God's sake! And with a corduroy jacket."

"Shhh," Blanche cautioned.

"I already don't like this guy," Mike said tightly. "I feel like turning around and going home."

"Don't be silly," Blanche said. "You haven't even met him yet. Besides, you're in charge of the choir."

"I've been threatening to resign, anyway," Mike muttered.

Blanche looked around at him. "You're kidding, right?"

Tess found the switch for the foyer light and flipped it on. Blanche and Mike turned, blinking. Clearly they hadn't heard Tess and Luke come in.

The four of them exchanged greetings and Blanche said, "Pastor Matt was looking for you a minute ago, Tess. I think he wanted you to have the honor of introducing Sherwood Draper."

Tess made a face. "Gee, and I missed it. Darn."

Through the door, they could hear Pastor Matt's muffled voice. He spoke in the same sonorous tone that he used in the pulpit. It was deeper and more vibrant than his everyday voice. Luke called it his preacher's voice.

Tess walked over to stand beside Blanche. Looking through the pane of glass, she noticed that Madison and Curt were sitting behind the Brookside twins and Eddie Zoller, in a pew about two-thirds of the way from the front. Boyd and Brenda, having turned around in their seats, talked in low voices to Madison and Curt. Then Eddie Zoller twisted around and added something that made Madison giggle. Tess was glad to see that the other young people weren't being standoffish with the new kids in town. It didn't appear that she would have to worry about their getting bored, at least not today.

Blanche said, "We can't hang around in the foyer all day. We better go in." She opened the door and started down the aisle. Mike hesitated, then followed and caught her hand, pulling her into a pew two rows behind Madison and Curt.

"Why do you want to sit way back here?" Blanche hissed.

"I'd like to assess the situation before I commit myself to anything." Mike muttered. "I've got a feeling this guy is trouble. I still may resign." He slumped down in the pew. Sighing, Blanche sat beside him. She shrugged off her coat and leaned forward, her hands on the back of the pew in front of her. Her head was cocked as she listened to the minister.

As Tess and Luke walked quietly toward the front, the

Chandlers entered the sanctuary and passed down the aisle on the other side of the center section of pews. Tess's gaze scanned the audience of about thirty people before returning to the minister.

The pastor, looking younger than his thirty-five years in jeans and a v-necked red sweater over a blue plaid shirt, stood in front of the raised platform, three steps up from the floor. On Sundays, the robed choir sat in rows at the back of the platform between the pulpit and the organ.

Sherwood Draper stood beside the minister, looking aloof and fondling his pipe with one hand. The other hand was tucked into the pocket of his corduroy jacket. He looked as though he were posing for *Gentlemen's Quarterly*.

Pastor Matt was explaining to the dauntless souls who'd braved the weather to gather in the front pews that Professor Draper had had an illustrious stage career in the U.S. and abroad. In his second career he had chosen to share his wealth of knowledge with aspiring young actors, first as director of a community theater group in Denver, more recently as head of the drama department at Colorado's Ulster College. Professor Draper, intoned the pastor, had had extensive experience in directing dramatic productions and pageants of all kinds and he was sure they all felt honored to be the fortunate recipients of Draper's vast store of knowledge.

Plainly the minister was determined to sell the audience on Draper's merits. Tess had rarely heard so much poetic license in so short a speech. As she and Luke reached Lily and Denny Brookside, who were seated on the aisle, she heard Denny mutter, "If he's so great, how come nobody ever heard of him?"

Lily silenced him with a glare.

"The reverend *is* laying it on a bit thick," Luke whispered near Tess's ear.

Tess watched anxiously as the Chandlers, who had hesitated in the aisle of the sanctuary, made their way to the front pew and sat down. Bill Chandler, a local insurance agent, put an arm protectively around Claire's shoulders. She turned her head to smile at him. Tess's anxiety eased a little. Perhaps Claire was actually going to swallow her pride and be at least semicooperative. Mavis Draper sat on the front pew, too, but several feet separated her from the Chandlers.

Tess's Aunt Dahlia and cousin Cinny sat together behind and to one side of the Chandlers. Tess and Luke slid into their pew. Dahlia reached for Tess's hand and squeezed it. Then she took Luke's hand and whispered, "Hello, you two." Dahlia's full-length fox coat was folded over the back of the pew. Dahlia loved that coat. Cinny, who refused to wear fur, had suggested that Dahlia might want to get herself a cloth coat. Dahlia had informed her daughter that it hadn't been politically incorrect to own a fur when she bought it, and she had no intention of leaving it in the closet just because a few people had gotten crazy over the subject. "These foxes have been dead for a long time," she'd said, "and leaving them in the closet won't resurrect them." Gamely, Cinny had tried to explain the thinking of the animal rights activists, but Dahlia had retorted, "When you stop buying leather shoes and purses, you can talk to me about it."

Dahlia was dressed in a lime green sweater with matching wool slacks. The outfit had designer label written all over it. As always, Dahlia's frosted hair was arranged perfectly.

Cinny, which was short for Hyacinth, leaned forward to smile at Tess and Luke. She still wore her hot pink down jacket, her long blond hair tucked under the collar. A knitted hunter green stocking cap and matching mittens lay in Cinny's lap.

"Aren't you opening the bookstore today?" Tess asked her cousin.

Cinny shook her head. "Not much point this morning. Maybe this afternoon."

Dahlia whispered in Tess's ear. "Did you know Pastor Matt brought this man in from Colorado for the pageant?"

Tess nodded and whispered back, "I found out yesterday. How do you think Claire's handling it?"

"So far, she's being very quiet," Dahlia murmured. Her eyebows arched up a notch. "Which in itself is troubling."

Good point. Tess hadn't thought of it that way.

Cinny leaned across her mother. "Can you see Claire's face?" she whispered to Tess. "I keep expecting her to blow any minute."

"Bite your tongue," Tess said. From where she sat, she had a good side view of Claire's pinched face, the mouth set in a hard, grim line, and realized her hope that Claire had decided to accept Draper gracefully was a bit optimistic. Claire was biding her time.

Having finally finished singing Draper's praises, Pastor Matt sat down beside Mavis. Draper tossed back his forelock dramatically and slowly scanned the faces turned toward him. Then he began to explain what he had in mind for the pageant, making several references to his London run in Hamlet with Richard Burton. Tess had the impression that he could go on like that all morning.

After twenty minutes, Tess believed that he *intended* to go on like that all morning. Around her, feet shuffled and somewhere behind her somebody muffled a yawn.

Finally, Elizabeth Purcell, a seventyish widow, interrupted Draper, having apparently come to the same conclusion as Tess—the only way to stop Draper's monologue was to interrupt.

"Let me see if I understand what you're saying, Professor Draper," Elizabeth said sweetly. "These little pantomimes you're describing—they will be modern interpretations of the Christmas story?" In spite of her soft tone, Elizabeth's face was flushed. Tess realized the woman was actually outraged, but struggling to remain calm.

Draper did not seem aware that he was dealing with an angry woman, though her reference to "little pantomimes" obviously rankled. "That's correct, madam," he said shortly, impatient at having the flow of his words interrupted by this nonentity of a person who obviously didn't know what she was talking about.

"So, Mary will be a modern young girl dressed"— Elizabeth's hand fluttered in mid-air—"well, the way young girls dress today, and, instead of the stable, she'll give birth in a hotel lobby?"

Looking bored with Elizabeth's persistence, Draper nodded.

"The Holiday Inn would be cute," Claire whispered to her husband, but loud enough to be heard by half of those present.

If Draper heard, however, he gave no sign. He turned away from Elizabeth, prepared to resume his lecture.

But Elizabeth wasn't finished. "And instead of the organ, there will be guitars and drums?" Elizabeth was the church organist.

Draper stuck the stem of his unlit pipe between his teeth and clamped down on it—hard. He looked down his nose at Elizabeth with an expression of exceedingly strained patience. Removing the pipe after a moment, he said, "Among other instruments." He turned away, determined to regain control of the session. "Now, where was I . . ."

Before Draper could continue, Elizabeth came to her feet. "Do you really think you can put together a band in the time we have before the pageant?"

"No, madam, I do not. I brought tapes with me."

Elizabeth abandoned her attempt to be civil. "Tapes? *Tapes* are downright tacky."

"You are entitled to your opinion." Pointedly, Draper turned his back on Elizabeth.

Elizabeth was undaunted. "Excuse me, but is this your idea of a joke or are you actually serious?"

Draper's startled gaze returned to her. It was beginning to dawn on him that she wasn't the sweet, little old lady he'd assumed she was, someone who could easily be brushed aside with a stern look from beneath that lock of dark hair. He tossed the forelock out of his eyes. "When it comes to my work, I'm not in the habit of joking. My ultimate goal is to make the program relevant to today.''

Elizabeth's hands gripped the back of the pew in front of her. The knuckles were white. ''Are you suggesting the Bible, as it's written, isn't relevant today?''

Draper exhaled a long breath and looked toward the vaulted ceiling.

Pastor Matt cleared his throat. ''Elizabeth, I'm sure that isn't what Professor Draper meant.''

Tess glanced at Claire Chandler and saw the grim line of her mouth relax as a faint, satisfied smile curved her lips.

''Pardon me, Pastor,'' Elizabeth snapped, ''but I assume he meant what he said, and *that's* what he said.''

''No, madam,'' Draper said. ''You misunderstood. Surely you can see that the suggestions I'm making are merely props, window dressing to engage the audience. The same Christmas story will still be told, the message will be the same.''

''I beg to differ,'' Elizabeth retorted. ''I was an elementary school teacher for thirty years, and children learn as much by what they see as by what they hear. In fact, they probably learn more that way. This updated, rock-and-roll version of the Christmas story will merely confuse them.''

''No one said anything about rock and roll!'' snapped Draper.

Elizabeth's voice rose higher. ''Furthermore, I can guarantee that it won't go over with the older members of this congregation—'' She glared at Pastor Matt as she added, ''—who, by the way, donate a good portion of the weekly contribution.''

Claire turned her head around to smirk at Tess, and Bill, Claire's husband, squeezed her shoulder as he bent over to whisper to her. Tess read his lips, and what Bill said was, ''Who does this guy think he is?''

Oh, fine, Tess thought. Remarks like that will only fuel Claire's indignation.

Pastor Matt cleared his throat and got reluctantly to his feet. "Perhaps we could reserve judgment until we have a couple of practices," he said tentatively, trying to walk the tightrope that had sprung up between Draper and some members of his audience. Pastor Matt appeared about to continue, but scanned the faces turned toward him and what he saw there seemed to change his mind. Abruptly, he sat back down.

"I have a question." The voice belonged to Diane Ferguson, who was seated behind Tess. "What about the children's portion of the program?" Diane was the mother of two preschoolers.

Draper blinked, throwing his head up and taking a step back, as though poleaxed by the question. "Children? I'm afraid there will be very few parts for young children in the pageant."

Following Elizabeth's example, Diane rose to her feet. She was frowning. "But the children always take part. They've been practicing their songs for weeks now."

Another young mother spoke up from the back of the sanctuary. It sounded like Pam Yoder. Tess hadn't noticed her when she came in. "The kids are also preparing a play," Pam said loudly. "They're very excited about it. In years past, Mike Tandy, dressed as Santa, came on stage with the kids at the end of their program and handed out Christmas stockings. They're expecting to see Santa this year, too."

"Santa!" Draper almost choked on the word and glanced beseechingly at Pastor Matt, who was suddenly intensely interested in a loose piece of yarn sticking out of his sweater sleeve. No help there. "As it happens," Draper went on, "I've had no experience working with children."

"Forgive me," Pam Yoder said, "but I can't believe you didn't expect to work with children. This congregation is full of young families. Surely Pastor Matt told you that."

"Perhaps," suggested Diane, "Claire Chandler could

take charge of that portion of the program. She's so good with the kids."

"She's always been in charge of the whole pageant before," Pam chimed in, "and done an excellent job."

Everybody looked at Claire, who continued to remain uncharacteristically silent, her head bowed modestly. There was an enigmatic smile on her face.

Definitely biding her time, Tess thought.

"Claire," Pastor Matt said, "would you mind very much supervising the children?"

Blinking at the pastor, as though she were surprised to be noticed, Claire idly fingered a wisp of light brown hair that had fallen across her cheek. "I'm not sure. I'd have to rearrange my schedule," she said thoughtfully, "because, of course, I was under the impression that my services wouldn't be needed this year."

"Nonsense, we need everybody's help." Pastor Matt was trying to sound hearty, but instead he succeeded in sounding thoroughly alarmed. Clearly, things weren't going according to expectations. Tess didn't feel much sympathy for him—he should have known better.

"How much time will be allotted to the children?" Claire asked, her eyes on Pastor Matt, but she was plainly aware of Draper, now standing stiffly in front of the assemblage, one hand gripping the bowl of his pipe, the other hand clenched at his side.

Pastor Matt looked to Draper for an answer. "I suppose," said Draper, his voice strained and grudging, "we could give them ten minutes at the end of the program."

Disgruntled murmurs came from the audience. "Ten minutes!" Diane exclaimed. "They could barely do three songs in that length of time. It's hardly worth getting them dressed up and bringing them down here."

"They've always had thirty or forty minutes before," added Pam. "And they should be the first thing on the program. They'll be tired and cranky if they have to wait till the end. And the parents will be livid. A lot of them only come to see their kids. The parents of the younger children usually leave as soon as the children are finished.''

"Leave?'' Draper looked appalled.

"The kids get bored,'' Diane added. "If they aren't taken out, they'll raise a fuss.''

"My word,'' said Draper, his voice agitated. "We simply can't have people traipsing out halfway through the program.''

"Perhaps we could put a guard on the door,'' Claire suggested with a pleasant smile for Draper.

Draper glared at her. "If the parents are in the habit of leaving after the children perform, that's even more reason for them to be last on the program.''

"Pastor Matt,'' Claire said, still in the same reasonable tone, "I'm sure *you* can explain to the parents why it's necessary for their little darlings to wait for an hour or two backstage, crying and scuffling and mussing their pretty clothes before they set foot on the stage.''

Pastor Matt's expression held an edge of panic, like an animal who's just discovered he's cornered with no way out. He studied a few of his parishioners' faces and saw what he had to do. He cast an apologetic look in Draper's direction. "I'm afraid they're right. We'd have chaos on our hands. I'm sorry, but we'll have to put the children on first.''

Red-faced, Draper rammed his unlit pipe into his jacket pocket so hard that Tess was sure he'd ripped out the lining. "Very well. We'll give them ten minutes at the beginning. But I must have one thing understood here and now. I will not tolerate interference with my artistic vision.''

Claire shook her head. "I'm afraid your artistic vision won't sell so well out here in the boonies. We're all a little backward, I suppose. Sorry, but if the kids only get ten minutes, I can't agree to be part of it. I can't fit *my* artistic vision into such a short time. Maybe dear Lily Brookside would like to supervise the children.''

"Me!'' Lily said shrilly. "Sherwood—er, Professor

Draper has already asked me to take part in the drama. I'm to play an angel.''

Claire shrugged. ''How very imaginative. Well, I'm sure Pastor Matt can find somebody.''

''We can't disappoint the children,'' Pastor Matt said hastily. ''We'll give them half an hour at the beginning of the program. And we'll reserve judgment on the pageant as a whole until we know for sure what Professor Draper has in mind. Will that do, Claire?''

Claire hesitated, as though in careful deliberation, then nodded. Tess had a suspicion that the thirty minutes allotted to the children would stretch into forty-five, with Claire in charge, possibly even an hour.

''That's unacceptable,'' sputtered Draper.

Before anybody could respond, Pastor Matt was on his feet, looking anxiously around the sanctuary. ''I'm afraid I have work to do. Oh, there you are, Blanche, hiding in the shadows.'' He grinned, letting her know he was only kidding. ''I'm sure you can assist Professor Draper in working out the logistics here.'' He glanced at Draper. ''My secretary will take care of any question or problem you have.'' Having created the problem, then, Pilate-like, washing his hands of it, Pastor Matt moved to the aisle. ''Kids,'' he said, indicating the small group of teenagers several pews back. ''I could use your help decorating the fellowship hall for the teen party. Come with me.''

He strode down the aisle, and was followed by Eddie Zoller, the Brookside twins, and Curt. Madison took a few steps down the aisle and hesitated near the front. ''Professor Draper?''

He turned toward her, and his expression shifted slowly from indignation to reflection as he studied her. It was the same way he'd looked at her at the breakfast table, as though he were overcome by a feeling of déjà vu, as though he was trying to place her. Then, recognition altered the look in his eyes.

''Professor Draper?'' Madison said again.

He brushed back his forelock with his hand. ''Sorry,

but I just realized who you remind me of. My sister.''

''Oh.'' Madison didn't seem to know how she was supposed to respond to that. ''Uh . . . I'd like to go and help decorate the fellowship hall if you don't need me right now.''

He seemed to shake off a heavy weight. ''It doesn't look as though we'll get to your part this morning, Madison.''

Madison brightened, glad to hear it. She hurried after Pastor Matt and the other teenagers.

Blanche Tandy passed her in the aisle, walking toward the front where she sat down at the end of the front pew. Draper, now seeming at a loss, looked over the rebellious little crew gathered before him. They gazed back at him, some combatively, others defensively or expectantly. All but Claire, who seemed lost in her own private thoughts. Revising the children's part of the pageant, Tess surmised, to make it more elaborate than ever before. Claire would make sure that the children's program outshone Draper's pageant.

''I think we should talk about the music,'' Blanche said.

''There's nothing to talk about. I have my tapes.''

Blanche swallowed and went on. ''In my opinion, the Christmas program simply wouldn't be right without the organ and some of the traditional carols.''

Draper closed his eyes as if praying for patience.

Blanche went on doggedly. ''We always sing a couple of carols where the audience joins in.''

Draper finally opened his eyes and looked at her. ''How charming.''

''Actually it is,'' Blanche retorted.

Draper merely waited for her to go on.

Blanche looked over her shoulder, craning her neck. ''You'll need to talk to my husband about the music. He's in charge of the choir. Mike?''

But the sanctuary door was already closing on a disgusted Mike Tandy.

"Excuse me," Blanche said and ran up the aisle to catch her husband before he followed through on his threat to go home.

*Chapter 6*

Blanche managed to catch Mike and drag him back into the sanctuary, but only as far as the back pew. Eventually, Draper spoke to Mike about the choir's contribution to the pageant and agreed that they could sing three traditional carols—"Silent Night," "O Little Town of Bethlehem," and "The First Noel" with the audience joining in if they felt like it. The choir, however, would not be a part of the pageant itself, but a sort of epilogue. They would take the stage at the end of the pageant and be last on the program.

As Dahlia said, "A sop to keep the peace. I can't believe it! The choir is being replaced by taped music. That's an insult!"

Draper ignored such grumblings, more concerned with finding enough players to perform in the pageant. It didn't help his mood any that Claire informed him they'd never had any problem getting enough players in past years. Draper tried to assign the casting job to Mike. Mike refused, and after a brief, unsatisfying conversation with Draper, Mike stomped out. Again.

"I've never seen Mike be so rude," Blanche said to Tess and Luke as they were leaving the church for a lunch break. It was anybody's guess how many of those assembled that morning would return for the first pageant practice after lunch.

Luke, who was walking behind the two women, observed, "Sherwood Draper's whole attitude is condescending. Mike's not the only one who's mad. I wouldn't be surprised to learn that Bill Chandler and Denny Brookside had formed a lynch party."

Blanche shook her head, as if in bewilderment. "At least Bill and Denny tried to be civil. Mike never even pulled down that faded old sweatshirt hood. Hardly said two words to the man. Just scowled while Draper talked, refused to look him in the eye, and then tore out of here like his pants were on fire."

"I agree with Luke," Tess said. "Mike had reason to be upset. For starters, the kids' program will take up the best part of an hour—"

Blanche darted an anxious glance at Tess. "Do you really think Claire would do that?"

"I really do," Tess said. "Say an hour for the kids, and if Draper's pageant can even be confined to an hour, I'll be surprised. That's at least two hours before anybody sees the choir. They've always had a major role in past pageants and Draper has cut their part to a few minutes and tacked it on the end of the program like an afterthought. Half the audience will have left by then and the other half will be desperate to go home. They will hardly feel like joining in a sing-along."

"I still say thirty minutes is plenty of time for the pageant," Blanche said.

"Tell that to Draper."

"I'll speak to Pastor Matt about it, but I doubt it'll do much good. I got the impression Draper will do what he wants to do."

"Like Claire," Tess added. "Irresistible force meets immovable object."

"Yes." Blanche gnawed worriedly on the inside of her cheek. "I'll think about that later. Right now I have to go and find Mike. The choir is supposed to meet with Draper some time this afternoon.'' Pulling on her gloves, she hurried up the aisle.

Dahlia and Cinny followed close behind Luke. ''What are your lunch plans, Tess?'' Dahlia asked.

''I'm not sure, Aunt Dahlia. I have to find Curt and Madison and see what they want to do.''

''I left a beef stew simmering in the crock pot at my house. Cinny and I are going there for lunch. You're all welcome to join us. You, too, Luke.''

''Stew sounds wonderful,'' Tess said. ''Just let me talk to the kids.''

Dahlia pulled her fox collar up around her face. ''We won't wait. Come on over if you want to. If not, that's okay, too.''

They had reached the foyer and Dahlia and Cinny headed for the parking lot. Putting on his gloves, Luke said, ''I'll go warm up the Jeep while you find Curt and Madison.''

The fellowship hall was in the basement. Tess exited the foyer through a north door which opened on a long hallway with classrooms lining it on both sides. The stairs to the basement were at the north end of the hall.

Tess found Madison and Boyd Brookside, seated at a long table, surrounded by rolls of red and green ribbon, crepe paper, pieces of shiny gold and silver paper, and small boxes of various colors of glitter. Boyd glued gold glitter to a row of big red bows while Madison cut lengths of red ribbon with wicked-looking giant shears.

Curt and Brenda stood at one side of the hall, handing bows and glittery cut-outs to Eddie, who perched atop a ladder and attached the decorations to the wall.

''Hey, guys, it's time for lunch,'' Tess said.

''Tell me about it!'' Curt said.

Madison looked up. ''Oh, hi, Tess.'' Not a trace of her earlier gloom remained.

''How'd pageant practice go?'' Brenda asked.

''We didn't really get into that yet,'' Tess said. ''Professor Draper assigned some of the roles and there's supposed to be a practice after lunch.''

Madison looked glum. "I guess that means I won't get to help down here this afternoon."

"The choir will practice sometime this afternoon, too," Tess said.

"That gets Brenda and Eddie and me, then," said Boyd, with a warm grin for Madison.

Those two seemed to be getting along famously.

"That just leaves me," Curt said. "I don't want to work down here by myself."

Madison laughed. "You're just scared to be alone." She looked at Tess. "Eddie has been telling us ghost stories."

"I'm not scared!" Curt insisted.

"Not even," Brenda hooted.

Curt made a face at her.

"Hey, Curt," said Eddie, "I made up those stories. The sanctuary isn't really haunted."

"I'll tell you what," Tess said. "The five of you can stay down here after lunch and I'll come and get you when you're needed. No point in sitting in a pew, waiting, when you could be finishing this." She glanced around. Twisted streamers of red and green crepe paper were draped from the light fixture in the center of the ceiling to the walls, all the way around. "This looks great. When's the teen party?"

"Friday night," Boyd said.

"It's a sock hop," Brenda added.

"Boyd and Brenda asked Curt and me to come with them," Madison said. "I need to shop for something to wear, Tess. I don't have anything dressy with me."

Tess didn't think you needed anything dressy for a sock hop, but didn't want to get into an argument with Madison, so she said, "Fine. We'll figure something out before Friday. Right now, Luke's waiting for us outside to take us to lunch."

"You go ahead, Tess," Madison said. "Pastor Matt's gone after pizza for all of us."

"He better get plenty," Curt said. "I'm starved!"

"You're always starved," Madison observed.

"How long has he been gone, anyway?" Curt asked.

Boyd looked at his watch. "Half an hour. He'll be back any minute."

"Don't you mean any day?" Eddie asked.

"No, really," Boyd said. "Pastor Matt doesn't want us to get away."

"Yeah, I guess you're right," Eddie said, "we're doing such an awesome job here, he'll want to keep us fed and happy."

"What he means," said Brenda, "is that Pastor Matt doesn't get the use of slave labor like this very often."

Boyd laughed. "Yeah, can't have the natives getting restless."

"That's fine, then," Tess said, glad to know that Pastor Matt would be back soon. "See you all this afternoon."

"Eddie and the twins are the leaders of the church's teen set," Dahlia said. "It's sweet of them to include Madison and Curt in the fun."

Dahlia, Cinny, Tess, and Luke were seated at Dahlia's kitchen table, lunching on hearty beef stew, cheese, and a variety of crisp crackers. Dahlia's husband, Maurice, had gone to the bank at nine that morning, as usual, and hadn't returned for lunch.

"I swear," Cinny said, "it's a miracle how that Eddie Zoller has changed since he went to live with Mike and Blanche. It's like he can't do enough to please them, especially Mike."

"The poor boy never had a father he could depend on before Mike," Dahlia said. "The Tandys have virtually saved Eddie Zoller's life."

"Obviously he appreciates it, too," Tess said.

"Speaking of teenagers," Dahlia said, "Curt and Madison are growing up so fast, I hardly recognized them."

"Hmm," Tess agreed. "I promised Curt we'd get a sled this afternoon, but he didn't mention that in the fellowship hall. I guess he's enjoying himself so much he forgot about it. As for Madison, she thinks Boyd's cute, and I got the distinct impression the feeling is mutual."

Luke reached for a handful of cheese crackers. "Young love."

Tess frowned. "Madison and Curt have been invited by Boyd and Brenda to attend the teen party Friday night. Zelda doesn't allow Madison to date—but I wouldn't exactly call that a date, would you, Aunt Dahlia?"

"No," Dahlia said. "There are always plenty of parents at those parties. Of course, Boyd has his own car, so you'll have to make sure he and Madison don't go off somewhere on their own."

Tess groaned. "I guess that means I have to go to the party, too."

"No," Cinny put in. "Several parents of teenagers will probably be chaperones. For sure the Brooksides will, they always are. Tell Lily—" She paused and chuckled. "Make that Denny—he's more dependable. Tell Denny that Madison isn't allowed to leave the fellowship hall until the party's over." She looked at Dahlia. "Mother used to do that to me all the time."

Dahlia cut her eyes around at her daughter "I didn't know you knew. I thought I was being so subtle about it."

"About as subtle as chaining me to the house," Cinny told her. Then she grinned at Tess. "Take a lesson, Tess. Make sure Madison doesn't know you've talked to Denny, or she'll be mortified. There's nothing more embarrassing than to be treated like a baby when you're fourteen and think you're grown up. I should know. Mother put a real crimp in my love life till I left for college."

"Poor darling," Dahlia murmured insincerely.

"Speaking of your love life," Luke put in, "are you still seeing Cody Yount?" Cody Yount was a young attorney who'd opened an office in Victoria Springs less than a year ago.

"Occasionally," Cinny said.

Dahlia cocked an elegantly arched brow. "They're practically joined at the hip. Every time I go over to Cinny's, Cody's there. Looking very much at home, I might add."

Tess watched Cinny wrinkle her nose at her mother. "Is this serious, Cinny?" Tess asked. Cinny went through boyfriends like salts through a midget, as Aunt Iris used to say. Come to think of it, though, Cinny had been seeing Cody for at least six months, which might be a record.

Cinny looked enigmatic. "We're quite fond of each other."

Coming from her cousin, Tess thought, that was nearly an engagement announcement. "You're welcome to bring him to Christmas dinner."

"Thank you, Tess. I've already invited him."

# Chapter 7

At one o'clock, Tess, Dahlia, and Cinny were back at the church. After receiving a phone call from his assistant, Luke had gone to his office, even though he'd agreed to play the innkeeper in the pageant. A few other people who'd been there that morning hadn't returned, either. Mavis Draper, the Chandlers, and the Brooksides were present, however, as were Elizabeth Purcell and Blanche and Mike Tandy. For some reason, Mike had decided to wear his Santa suit. He'd even powdered his beard and moustache and perched a pair of wire-framed glasses with clear lenses on his nose. Realizing that the costume would be a constant reminder of the children's program, Tess suspected Mike had worn it to irritate Draper.

Blanche was certainly irritated, but not, at the moment, with Draper. "I don't know why Mike insisted on coming in that garb," she whispered to Tess, as Mike strolled down the aisle calling, "Ho, ho, ho!"

"I think he's making a statement," Tess whispered back.

Blanche rolled her eyes. Mike was in an uncharacteristically rebellious mood, and it was plain Blanche didn't know how to handle it. "I begged him to come back after lunch, but now I almost wish he'd go on to the store," she muttered, looking around the sanctuary. "Less than a quarter of the choir is here. Mike will have to call evening practices."

Draper stared hard at Mike for a long moment, then evidently decided to ignore him. "I'd like those who have roles in the pageant to come up on the stage, please."

Lily Brookside jumped up and hurried forward. She was followed less enthusiastically by other players, including Mavis Draper, who'd been drafted to stand in for the innkeeper's wife, or more accurately the hotel manager's wife, until somebody could be found for the role. Tess had turned it down, saying she would have too much else to do.

Tess, who was seated on the front pew, stood up. "Professor, Luke Fredrik, the innkeeper, had to go to his office. He said he'd get here later if he could."

Draper, who had started up the stairs to the stage, whipped around to stare at Tess. "Ach!" He slapped his forehead with the heel of his hand. "That makes me insane!"

Tess didn't think that deserved a response.

Draper looked harried. "I must insist that you people take this seriously. I can't have you showing up for practice only when you feel like it."

Tess shrugged and sat down. He could take it up with Luke.

Gaining the stage, Draper surveyed his players for a moment, then asked sharply, "Where is Madison?"

Tess jumped back up. She'd forgotten about Madison. "She's downstairs. I'll get her."

"While you're at it," Draper barked, "ask one of those young men to come and play the innkeeper."

Loud music poured up from the basement. Tess hurried down the stairs. The music was coming from a portable tape player which sat on one end of the table where Madison and Boyd had been working earlier. Now all five young people were gathered at the table, three empty pizza boxes between them.

"Where's Pastor Matt?" Tess yelled over the music.

"He went to his office," Brenda yelled back.

"Could you turn that music down a little?" Tess shouted.

Eddie got up and turned it off.

"Madison, pageant practice is starting."

She made a face and got slowly to her feet. It was clear that being in the pageant had slipped below hanging out with these young people on her priority list.

"Boyd or Eddie," Tess said, "would one of you come up and play the innkeeper until Luke gets here?"

"I'll do it," Boyd said quickly.

"Let's all go," said Eddie. "We can't do anything else here right now, anyway."

As they traipsed up the stairs, Tess, who'd fallen in behind Madison, saw the top half of the big shears she'd been using earlier protruding from the hip pocket of her sister's jeans. As they gained the hallway, Tess reached over and extracted the shears. "I'll take care of these," she said, "before you stab yourself in the behind."

Madison looked over her shoulder at Tess and giggled. "Oops. I forgot I still had those."

Back in the sanctuary, Tess laid the shears beside her on the front pew. Eddie, Brenda, and Curt filed into the second pew, while Madison and Boyd went up on the stage.

Tess leaned over to ask Blanche, "Where's Draper?"

"Backstage," Blanche told her. "When he said they'd have to practice till dinnertime, Claire informed him the children were coming to run through their program at three." She shook her head helplessly. "I'm sure she didn't check with Draper first. It looks like Claire is going to do everything she can to interfere with the pageant. Draper is furious."

Tess noticed that Draper wasn't the only person who'd disappeared. "Where's Claire?"

"When Draper stormed backstage, Lily ran after him. Then Draper's wife got up and went after them. That's when Claire decided to go back, too, figuring the more the merrier, I suppose. Then Mike followed Claire."

Onstage, Boyd and Madison stood to one side, talking in low tones. The other players merely stood or sat mutely on stage, waiting.

Tess could hear no voices coming from backstage. "What are they *doing* back there?" she asked.

Blanche looked worried. "I wish I knew. The mood Mike's in, he's liable to throw a punch at Draper if he gets ugly with Claire about the children's program."

Tess got up. "Let's go find out what's going on."

"Do you think we should?"

"Why not? Pastor Matt left you in charge, and I'm your assistant."

"Okay. Let's go.

No one was in sight backstage. The door to one of the two changing rooms was closed. Tess heard muffled voices coming from behind it. She opened the door.

"—will not tolerate this. I'm in charge here!" Draper was saying. He stood in the center of the small room, his face red, his ascot askew. Mavis hovered anxiously at his elbow. Claire and Mike leaned against one wall, muttering to each other.

"After today, practices for the children's program and the choir will simply be worked in around pageant practice," Draper said, looking pointedly at Claire and Mike. Neither responded.

Lily walked over to stand in front of Draper. "Don't let it upset you, Sherwood," she said placatingly. "People don't like change. Give them a chance to get used to the idea of a professional pageant director." Ignoring Claire's muffled snort, Lily reached up with both hands to straighten Draper's ascot.

Mavis snatched Lily's arm. "Get your hands off my husband!"

Startled, Claire and Mike turned to watch the little tableau. Lily stepped back and shook off Mavis's hand. "I was only—"

"I know what you were doing!" Mavis said. "And you'd better stop fawning over Sherwood or else!"

Lily laughed nervously. "Or else? Really, you sound like a B movie. You're making a spectacle of yourself, Mavis."

"I could take lessons from you in that department," Mavis shot back. Her face was flushed and she looked ready to scratch Lily's eyes out any minute.

"Be quiet, Mavis!" Draper stormed. "You're not needed here. Wait for me in the sanctuary." His glance fell on Tess and Blanche, who stood in the open doorway. "What do *you* want?"

Tess stepped aside to let Mavis leave. The woman's face was mottled and, deep in her eyes, fury smoldered. Tess wondered whom she was more angry with—her husband or Lily Brookside.

Blanche said, "We wanted to see if we could be of help. Everybody's waiting for you."

"That's what actors do," Draper snapped. "Wait for the director. Sometimes they wait for hours."

"I wouldn't count on these actors doing that," Claire put in, examining her fingernails idly. "After all, they're not *professionals*. I don't think they'll put up with some temperamental junior college teacher's abuse."

"It may surprise you to learn, Mrs. Chandler, that I couldn't care less what you think. As for you two"—he gestured toward Tess and Blanche—"you are not needed here, either. Lily, please wait outside the room. You, too, Mrs. Chandler. I'd like a word with each of you alone. I'll speak to Mr. Tandy first."

The four women filed out and Draper closed the door. Claire walked a few steps and leaned back against the wall. Lily stepped to one side of the door. Blanche hesitated. "This isn't going to work, Lily."

"Yes, it will," Lily said shrilly, "if everybody will stop being so stupid and—and childish."

"You mean childish like Mavis Draper?" Claire inquired. "Imagine, getting upset because another woman's after her husband."

Lily whirled around. "Nobody's talking to you, Claire!"

Claire shrugged carelessly. "You know, Lily, if you're going to flirt with other women's husbands, you should learn to do it when their wives aren't around."

"I was merely straighting his ascot!"

"Of course." Claire smirked.

"Furthermore," Lily flared, "I don't need any advice from you, of all people."

"What's that supposed to mean?"

"It means that you've been trying to besmirch my name ever since I got involved at church."

Claire snorted. "Funny, I thought you didn't need any help. You do such a good job of that all by yourself."

Lily stomped her foot. "Shut up! Just shut up!"

Walking toward the stage, Tess and Blanche finally got out of hearing range. "Those two cause enough problems without tossing Sherwood Draper into the mix," Blanche muttered.

Tess sighed. "I know."

Blanche lowered her voice. "What's with Mavis Draper?"

"Between you and me, Blanche, I think the good professor is a womanizer."

Blanche nodded. "Explains why his wife reacted so violently to another woman touching his ascot."

Tess sighed. "You're right about one thing. This doesn't seem to be working."

"Do you think it would help if we talked to Pastor Matt?"

Tess sighed again. "Let's see how the rest of the day goes first. If things don't improve, we'll talk to him tomorrow."

They walked out on the stage. "Professor Draper will be with us in a minute," Blanche announced.

Tess returned to her seat. Mavis sat at the end of the pew, watching the stage anxiously. Leaning toward Tess, she asked, "Where's Sherwood?"

"He wanted to talk to the other three alone," Tess told her.

A few minutes later, Mike Tandy and Claire Chandler walked out from behind the stage. Claire slid into a pew beside her husband three rows from the front. Mike sat down beside Blanche.

Mavis's gaze remained glued to the stage entrance.

After several moments, when Draper and Lily still had not returned, Mavis hissed, "I warned her!" Her hands were clenched into tight balls, and the tendons in her neck stood out like ropes.

Tess feared she would pop a blood vessel any minute. "I don't think you should take Lily's behavior too seriously," she ventured.

Mavis stared at her as though Tess had suddenly started babbling incoherently. "Oh," she flung back, "what do you know about it?" Then she jumped up and ran backstage.

Claire watched Mavis scurry from sight, then took a small memo pad from her purse and began making notes. Tess thought she was perfectly calm until she noticed the hard set of Claire's jaw. It looked like concrete. Bill kept sending her questioning glances, of which Claire took no notice.

Blanche was talking in low, but urgent tones to her husband. Mike sat with his head bowed. Tess couldn't tell if he was listening to Blanche or pouting and ignoring her.

Just when Tess thought things couldn't get any worse, Denny Brookside muttered, "What the hell . . ." He got up and followed Mavis backstage. Tess wondered who was minding the grocery store. Denny didn't usually hang around the church.

Shortly, Denny stalked back into the sanctuary, holding himself as stiff as a yardstick. He was followed by Lily who looked disturbed and more subdued than Tess had ever seen her. Denny, grim-faced, returned to a pew, while Lily remained on stage with her back to the audience, her head lowered. Draper appeared on stage a few moments later. His hair was mussed and one end of his silk ascot hung from his jacket pocket. His forelock drooped over his eyes, but he didn't bother throwing it back. He was pale, like someone who'd just received a severe shock.

Moments later, Mavis came out, walked tensely across the stage and down the steps to her seat, chin up, staring forward, over the heads of the people in the pews.

Good grief, Tess thought, what on earth happened backstage?

The afternoon went downhill from there.

Luke didn't make it back for practice. Draper tried to make the best of the partial cast he had to work with, but he was in danger of losing even those players. He was so short-tempered he barked at people right and left and clapped his palm to his forehead a lot.

Eventually, the cast members learned what was expected of them and Draper seemed to calm down. A few minutes before three o'clock, he said, "All right. Let's walk through it from the beginning. Joseph, remember, Mary is your young wife and you're very protective of her. Try to loosen up a little."

The chubby man who played Joseph blushed, but moved a cautious step closer to Madison, who had really gotten into her part and earned the only compliment of the afternoon from Draper. The man playing Joseph seemed in awe of Madison's tender years combined with her total lack of self-consciousness.

At that moment, children's voices were heard in the foyer and Tess noticed that Claire had left her seat. Then the sanctuary doors flew open and Claire tripped down the aisle, followed by an army of preschoolers, chattering and sniffling from the cold and singing in their high little voices.

Claire was leading them in "Jingle Bells."

"O, God!" Draper moaned as Claire started up on stage with the children. "Is it three o'clock already?" He frowned at his watch. "People!" he shouted over the children's voices to his cast. "Don't anybody leave! Pageant practice isn't over. We still have so much work to do I don't even know when I'll sleep. We practice as soon as we can get possession of the stage."

# Chapter 8

Backstage, Mavis Draper retreated to one of the changing rooms, shut the door behind her and locked it by pushing in a little button beside the doorknob. Her mouth was as dry as cotton. Her throat was tight. Her heart felt like a sponge that had absorbed so much water it weighed twenty pounds and was trying to beat hard enough and fast enough to get rid of some of the liquid before the weight stopped its beating altogether.

She stared at herself in the full-length mirror attached to the wall and told herself to get a grip. Her lipstick had been eaten away, and she'd wiped off most of the mascara she had so carefully applied that morning. Now she looked waxen and lashless, like a doll abandoned by a child after she'd scraped off all the painted-on facial features. She hated to see herself like this but could not summon the energy to apply new lipstick and mascara. What was the point?

She pushed up her glasses with one finger on the nose piece and closed her eyes. But all she could see behind her eyelids were Sherwood and Lily Brookside, embracing, the way she'd found them earlier, in this very room. If she hadn't walked in on them, they'd have been wallowing on that couch against the wall next. They hadn't even bothered to lock the door.

She reached under her tunic and pulled out the big pair of shears she'd taken from the front pew where someone had discarded them. The blades were sharp and pointed on the ends. She gazed at the shears, wondering why she had taken them. What had she meant to do with them?

All right, she admitted to herself, she had had a thought about that. Not that she would really carry it out. Actually, it was more of a wish than an intention. When she'd touched the shears, an image had flashed across her mind, an image of Lily Brookside, fallen on her face, her carefully coiffed black hair in shaggy disarray, the long sharp blades buried in her back.

And blood everywhere.

An ordinary pair of shears, really, but they felt like a giant scorpion in her hand. She flung them down on the worn old couch, the only piece of furniture in the room.

She hated Lily Brookside, as she had hated many women before Lily. But she had never truly despised her husband until today. When she'd opened the door to find Sherwood and Lily, pawing at each other like a couple of oversexed adolescents, she'd felt thrown back in time. How often had she found Sherwood in similar situations? And what good did it do to follow him around? What had she hoped to accomplish by coming to Victoria Springs?

Nothing had changed, and yet, all at once, everything had changed. Because this time her perceptions of the whole world seemed to shift, especially her perception of her husband. For the first time in her marriage, she didn't try to make a single excuse for him and put the blame for his behavior on a woman. If they didn't come looking for him, he'd go looking for them.

Something was missing in Sherwood that most other men had, something vital that had to do with character and principles. It came to her then that she could not spend the rest of her life trailing after Sherwood to keep him away from other women. More than that, she no longer wanted to.

Her marriage was over. Finished. While the knowledge filled her with sorrow and a sense of having wasted half her life, there was also a kind of calm, too. A calm that came from having run out of options and knowing finally what she had to do.

Tess stayed around through the children's play practice, another pageant rehearsal, and finally choir practice. She spent part of the time in Blanche's office, calling around town to line up the few props that would be needed for the pageant. The costumes would be easy. Most of the actors would wear street clothes, so the church wouldn't have to rent costumes this year.

At four, a few more choir members began to arrive. By the time the stage was available, it was after five and more than half the choir was present. Elizabeth Purcell, the organist, took her place and the choir practiced entering and leaving the stage in correct order, then ran through the three carols they were to sing in the program.

"The First Noel" would be the last piece on the program, and the audience would be encouraged to join the choir in singing it—that is, whatever was left of the audience by then.

Several times as the choir practiced, Draper paced impatiently up one aisle, passed through the foyer, and came back down another aisle. When Mike gave the choir a fifteen-minute break, Draper disappeared backstage and the choir members dispersed to get a drink or use the rest room.

The choir seemed revived when they reassembled on stage and the practice went more smoothly. As they practiced the last carol, the old, familiar words rang loudly through the sanctuary.

*The first noel, the angels did say*
*'Twas to certain poor shepherds*
*in fields where they lay.*

*In fields where they lay, keeping their sheep*
*On a cold winter's night that was so deep.*
*Noel, noel.*
*Noel, noel.*
*Born is the king of Israel.*

Tess and Blanche timed everything. As best they could estimate, the program would last for close to three hours. That was twice as long as previous pageants. They would definitely have to talk to Pastor Matt tomorrow. If he insisted on keeping Draper, he would have to prevail on the man to shorten the pageant. Several of the scenes Draper planned could be eliminated, Tess thought, without hurting the pageant, though she knew Draper would resist any adjustments to his artistic vision. Should she try talking to Draper herself? She'd see what Blanche thought.

She looked around for Blanche, who had disappeared while the choir was on its break. Perhaps she was in the foyer. Tess hurried up the aisle.

Silently she pushed through the foyer door. Bill Chandler, standing beside the overcoats hanging from hooks along one wall, reached into his coat pocket and brought out a box of cough drops and a folded piece of paper. Frowning, he opened the paper, stared at it briefly, and, still frowning, shrugged, crumpled it, and walked over to a trash container in the corner. He tossed in the crumpled paper, turned, and saw Tess.

"Oh, hi. Didn't hear you come in." He held up the box. "My throat's feeling scratchy." He opened the box and extracted a cough drop.

"I'm looking for Blanche. Have you seen her?"

"Not in the last few minutes. Sorry." He popped the cough drop into his mouth and returned to the sanctuary.

Choir practice ended as Tess followed Bill Chandler back into the sanctuary. She hadn't seen Pastor Matt all afternoon, so she'd better find out if the Drapers had transportation back to Iris House—after she found Madison and Curt, who'd left the sanctuary when the choir took the stage.

Strains of "The First Noel" lingered in Tess's mind as she retrieved her purse from the front pew and went in search of her siblings.

*Chapter 9*

Lily and Denny Brookside stood in the foyer, waiting for the twins, who'd gone to the basement to get their coats. Or rather, Denny was waiting for the twins. Lily hadn't given Boyd and Brenda a thought since Mavis Draper had opened that changing room door at the very worst possible moment, and then had refused to listen to any explanations, saying, "You disgust me! I could kill the both of you!" It had been a meaningless little kiss, for God's sake.

Then Denny had appeared behind Mavis, and Lily had been sure she would tell Denny what she'd seen. But Mavis hadn't. She'd walked away without another word. Lily had thought she was home free, but as the afternoon dragged on, she had become convinced that Denny had come backstage in time to see what Mavis saw, or perhaps he'd only heard what she'd said to her husband and Lily and had drawn his own conclusion. At any rate, his face was fixed in a rigid sort of expressionlessness, like a corpse, and he had not spoken to Lily since.

Lily didn't know what to do. Never had her husband treated her like this. Good old dependable Denny was not himself at all and a painful knot had formed in Lily's stomach.

While the choir was practicing, she'd sat down beside Denny and made some comments about the

pageant. He'd glanced at her stonily, then got up and went
backstage, for what reason, Lily couldn't imagine. Denny
had refused even to look at her for the rest of the afternoon, just as he was doing now, standing as far away from
her as the small foyer allowed, one shoulder propped
against the wall, arms folded across his broad chest. She'd
give anything to know what he was thinking.

When Tess Darcy came into the foyer, Denny suddenly
straightened up and walked out of the foyer into the hallway where the classrooms were located. Lily watched him
uneasily. Where on earth was Denny going now?

Lily had gone from a desperate need for Denny to talk
to her to fear of what he would say when he did. She had
never seen Denny like this before and she had no idea
how to handle it.

She was certain about one thing. This whole fiasco was
a big mistake. She would give anything not to have suggested to Pastor Matt that he hire Sherwood to direct the
pageant. For the first time in her twenty-one-year marriage, she could not picture the future. And she was afraid.

Blanche, in the walk-in closet off the foyer, examined
the winter choir robes to see which were in need of repairs
or cleaning. Mike had gathered up his music, returned it
to its folder, and had gone downstairs to leave it in the
tiny cubbyhole of a room which held the file cabinet
where they kept all the sheet music.

At first, while the choir had been practicing onstage,
Sherwood Draper had paced back and forth, up one aisle
and down the other. Blanche supposed he was listening
and passing judgment on the quality of the singing. From
the closet, she could not be seen from the foyer, but she
heard Draper every time he passed through. Once, he'd
muttered to himself something that sounded like "Oh, my
God!"—apparently Draper's capsule critique of the choir.
Later, he'd paused for several moments in the foyer, and
she was tempted to peek out at him. But as she turned

around, the footsteps had resumed, and she'd heard him going back into the sanctuary.

Draper hadn't come through the foyer again, but several other people had. Blanche eased the closet door nearly closed, so as not to be distracted from her task. Ten minutes passed as she worked and, finally, the foyer was quiet again. Blanche picked up the three robes she'd tossed over a chair and rolled them into a ball to take to the cleaners tomorrow. Then she closed the closet door and almost ran into Tess Darcy, who'd evidently just come out of the sanctuary.

"Oops," Blanche gasped. "You startled me, Tess."

"Sorry. I was looking for you, though. Do you think we ought to talk to Professor Draper this evening about shortening the pageant?"

Blanche glanced toward the sanctuary doors. "I don't think I can face another confrontation today. Let's do it first thing tomorrow."

"Okay," Tess agreed, seeing that Blanche did indeed look extremely tired. She phoned Luke, then found Curt and Madison in the basement with the Brookside twins and told them it was time to leave.

"We'll be up in a sec," Madison said.

Tess went back to the sanctuary in search of the Drapers, noticed a few scraps of paper on the floor between pews and was picking them up when Madison and Curt bounded down the aisle.

"Boyd and Brenda invited us to go sledding tomorrow if school's still out," Madison said breathlessly, evidently forgetting that she'd scoffed at Curt's enthusiasm for sledding at breakfast. Of course, Boyd Brookside hadn't been in the picture then. "What time am I supposed to be here for practice?" Madison asked.

Wadding the accumulated litter in both hands, Tess straightened up. "I don't know. You'll have to ask the professor."

"I wish I hadn't agreed to be in the stupid pageant," Madison muttered as she scanned the sanctuary, which was unoccupied now except for the three of them.

"Professor Draper praised your acting," Tess reminded her.

"Big deal," she muttered irritably. What a difference in her attitude a few hours had made.

"Curt," Tess said, "it's so late, I'm afraid we won't find a place to buy a sled this evening."

"That's okay. Boyd and Brenda have two sleds."

"Where's the professor?" Madison asked.

"I'm wondering that myself," Tess said. "I saw him go backstage a good while ago. Maybe he's still there." She hadn't seen Mavis in a long time, either, and wondered if she was backstage with her husband. There could be others backstage, as well. People had been wandering in and out of there all afternoon.

"I phoned Luke," Tess said, "and he's coming to pick us up. I don't know where Pastor Matt is, so I'd better see if the Drapers need a ride back to Iris House."

At that moment, Mavis Draper walked into the sanctuary from the foyer. She must have passed up the aisle while Tess was bending over, picking up litter, because the Brooksides were the only ones out there when Tess came back from the basement. Mavis blinked, trying to adjust her vision to the dim sanctuary where somebody had turned off most of the lights.

Tess thought Mavis looked dreadful, ashen and disoriented, like a person recovering from a long illness. Coming down the aisle, she touched the back of every pew she passed, as if for support. Madison and Curt watched her progress curiously.

"I'm looking for Pastor Matt," Mavis said.

"He may have gone to the hospital," Tess said. "A couple of our members were admitted yesterday. Or he could still be in his office." It wouldn't surprise Tess in the least if the pastor had forgotten he'd brought the Drapers to the church and ought to see that they had a way back to Iris House. "I was about to look for *you*," Tess said, "to see if you need to ride back with us."

"I suppose I do," Mavis said.

"Is your husband still backstage?" Tess asked.

Mavis frowned. "I didn't see him—when I was back there. I don't know where he's gone. I don't think we should worry about him. He'll get a ride." Tess wondered if he'd already gotten a ride as she'd heard nothing from backstage. From the silence, they could be the only people left at the church.

"I'm very tired," Mavis said. "I need to get back to Iris House and lie down."

Tess hesitated. "I'll just check backstage first. The professor could still be here somewhere." She went up the stairs to the stage, followed closely by Madison and Curt.

Stepping through the gap in the back curtains, Tess glanced both ways but saw no one. "Professor Draper," she called.

"If Pastor Matt went to the hospital," Curt said, "maybe the professor went with him."

"Wouldn't he have told somebody that he was leaving?" Tess murmured. She noticed that both changing room doors were closed and went to the nearest door to open it. The room was empty except for a sagging folding chair in one corner, but the light was still on. She turned out the light. Then, startled by a sound behind her, whirled around. Mavis Draper had followed them backstage.

"I don't think he's here," Mavis said.

"Doesn't look like it," Tess agreed. "Are you sure he didn't tell you he was leaving?"

Mavis shook her head. "No."

"Don't you think that's odd?"

She thought about it for a moment, then shook her head. "He might have wanted to be alone after what—" She halted and looked away from Tess. "Sometimes," she murmured, "he goes off by himself."

It seemed to Tess there was a world of pain behind that statement. "Where do those other two doors go?" Curt asked.

"That one leads outside behind the church," Tess said.

The professor could have left by that door, but why would he? "Behind the other door is another changing room, but if he was in there, he'd have heard me call his name."

Curt took a step toward the door.

"Go ahead," Tess said. "Check it out, anyway." She had just remembered that there was a couch in that changing room. "Maybe he's fallen asleep."

Curt walked to the door, his boots thumping loudly on the wood floor, and opened it. "It's dark in here," he said. "Where's the light?"

"To the left of the door," Tess said.

He felt around on the wall and flipped on the switch. Tess saw him freeze. Then he whirled around, his eyes as big as frisbees. "Tess!" His voice wobbled up an octave at the end. "Tess, come here quick!"

His sudden urgency made Tess run. She heard Madison clacking in the too-big boots right behind her. Mavis Draper did not move.

Curt stepped out of the doorway and leaned against the wall just outside it. Tess brushed past him and stepped into the changing room.

Sherwood Draper lay on the floor on his stomach, next to the couch, his face turned toward the door. His eyes were closed. A circle of wet, fresh blood soaked the back of his corduroy jacket. One blade of a pair of large shears was buried to the hilt in the center of the bloody circle. The shears looked like the ones Tess had taken from Madison and left on the front pew hours ago.

Madison pushed into the room behind Tess. Frozen, Tess hadn't thought to stop her. She couldn't look away from Sherwood Draper, and her mind was racing. Mavis Draper had seemed anxious to leave the church. She'd seemed to think, or wanted Tess to, that her husband was already gone. She'd even said he wasn't backstage.

All of this sped through Tess's mind in a flash and then Madison shrieked and stumbled from the room.

Tess thought she saw Draper's hand twitch. She made

herself walk forward and bend over him. Draper's eyelids fluttered.

"He's still alive. Curt," Tess said urgently, "go out to the foyer and call nine-one-one. Then go outside and tell everybody who's still around to stay till the police come."

She pressed two fingers against Draper's neck just below his jaw and felt a faint, erratic pulse. "Hang on, Professor. We're calling an ambulance."

His eyes opened. For one moment, he seemed to focus on Tess, and then beyond her to the doorway where Madison hovered, her hand over her mouth, her eyes wide with horror.

Draper made a strangled sound and Tess leaned closer. "Who did this to you, Professor?"

"Nancy," he whispered, and then what sounded like, "Howard." As Tess watched, the light went out of his eyes, and the faint pulse beneath her fingers stopped.

Her thoughts raced. CPR . . . she'd seen it done, though she'd never administered it herself. But she had to try. First she had to turn him over. Thinking of fingerprints, she reached out to grip the shears below the handles, where the blades were joined.

"Tess?" Mavis stepped past Madison into the room, halted in her tracks, and started screaming.

*Chapter 10*

Later, Tess would wish that she'd been quick-witted enough to immediately ask Madison to open the backstage door which led outside. She might have seen the killer leaving, provided the killer *had* left the church, and that that had been his means of escape. By the time the ambulance arrived and a paramedic took over what turned out to be the futile task of trying to resuscitate Sherwood Draper, it was far too late.

Then the police came, secured the crime scene, and looked behind the church, where they found footprints in the snow. The problem was, there were footprints on top of footprints, none of them very clear, and none could be tracked to the backstage door because, by that time, the sun had been shining all afternoon, and the snow on the walk leading to the door had turned to slush. And then, it turned out, that the teenagers had played in the snow behind the church during the afternoon, and their footprints were everywhere, too.

Besides, as Tess kept reminding herself, if the killer was somebody involved in the Christmas program, he or she could as easily have left through the sanctuary and nobody would have thought a thing about it. People had been backstage, on stage,

86

and walking up and down the aisles of the sanctuary all day.

Thinking back, Tess couldn't remember seeing Draper since the recess in the choir practice when he'd gone backstage. Perhaps he'd decided to take a nap, could even have been asleep when his attacker found him in the changing room. Draper could have lain there, moving in and out of consciousness, for some time before he was found. Had he been trying to call for help as Tess wandered around the sanctuary, picking up litter and humming "The First Noel"?

Which had turned out to be the last noel for Sherwood Draper.

These thoughts scrambled through Tess's head as she sat in the front pew with the Brooksides, the Tandys, the Chandlers, and the five teenagers. As it turned out, the church hadn't been virtually deserted, after all. All of these people had been there, in various places, when the body was found. Luke had arrived seconds after the police. Pastor Matt had come out of his office and had taken Mavis Draper, who was in no shape to be questioned immediately, back to Iris House.

The body had been removed to the morgue and Andy Neill, the officer in charge while Chief Desmond Butts vacationed in Florida, had instructed those present to stay for brief preliminary questioning. Neill questioned them as a group and asked them to recount their movements during the hours leading up to the discovery of the body. He also wanted to know when and where, to the best of their recollection, they had last seen Sherwood Draper. Nobody had seen him after he'd gone backstage during choir practice. At least, nobody admitted it.

Andy Neill took careful notes on the interviews and then dismissed them, saying he'd probably want to get back to all of them later. As Tess rose to follow the others out of the sanctuary, Neill said, "Tess, could I talk to you a minute?"

Tess sat back down and waited for the others to file out.

"When's Chief Butts due back?" she asked.

The young officer raked back a shock of straw-colored hair and tugged on one jug ear. "Not till after Christmas. I'm hoping I can wrap up this investigation before he gets home. I'd sure like for him to see how well I handled the job while he was gone."

Neill lowered his long, lanky body into the front pew beside Tess. "Thanks for staying, Tess."

"Sure."

"You know anything else you could share with me?" Neill asked with some anxiety.

Tess felt sorry for him. He was so eager to impress his boss that he was actually asking for Tess's help. Butts would censure him severely if he knew that. Butts had recommended, more than once, that she keep her nose out of police business. "You're not suggesting I'm withholding information, are you?"

"I didn't say that," Neill said hastily, "but I've noticed in the past that you're—er, sort of observant."

"You mean nosey?"

"Not at all, Tess. Not at all."

She laughed. "I'm teasing you, Andy. But you know your boss would say I'm nosey."

He grinned sheepishly. "Chief Butts made me acting chief in his absence, so I gotta use my own judgment."

Of course, Butts hadn't expected anything as serious as murder to occur during the off-season.

Neill frowned worriedly. "I know you said you never met the victim before he showed up at your bed and breakfast." He waved toward the back of the sanctuary where the others had just filed out. "And they didn't know him, either."

"Well—" Tess didn't want to cause trouble for anyone, but Neill already knew that what he'd just said wasn't strictly true. The Brooksides had admitted they'd become acquainted with Draper in Colorado. But maybe he'd forgotten. "I believe the Brooksides met him last year in Vail."

"Right." He nodded once. "That makes four people who already knew Sherwood Draper before he ever set foot in Victoria Springs. Lily and Denny Brookside, and their twins. As far as we know. I'll talk to the others tomorrow." He fished a small spiral notebook from his shirt pocket, flipped it open, and handed it to Tess. "Those are the names of people who were at the church some time today, but had left before the body was discovered." Neill had been given the names earlier by those people he'd already questioned. "Would you see if I've missed anyone?"

Tess read through the list. "I think that's everybody. If I remember anyone else later, I'll let you know."

He put the noteback back in his pocket.

"You didn't mention the person who knew Professor Draper far better than anyone else. His wife."

"Yeah," Neill said. "But right now, let's talk about Lily and Denny Brookside. You could cut the tension between those two with a knife. What's their problem?"

Tess sighed. She might as well tell him. It would all come out, anyway. "I believe Denny thought Lily and the professor were—well, flirting with each other."

He leaned closer and said in a confidential tone, "Wouldn't be the first time for Lily, would it?"

"I wouldn't know," Tess said primly.

"Wonder if Draper had a wandering eye, too," Neill mused.

"I—"

"I know. You want to be loyal to your guests. I'll ask his wife when I talk to her tomorrow morning. You can tell her I'll drop by Iris House between eight and ten. You can also tell her I'd appreciate her not making any plans to leave town for a couple of days."

"All right."

Neill rested his elbows on his knees and stared at the floor for a moment. "About those shears. You say you laid them on this front pew around one o'clock. When was the next time you noticed them?''

"Yes, I put them there as soon as the afternoon pageant practice started, thinking I'd return them later to the basement where the teenagers had been using them. But I forgot about it. I've tried and tried to remember when I next saw them," Tess said. "I think I saw them again not long after I put them down. One-thirty, maybe. After that, I don't remember seeing them again. But I wasn't looking for them, and I had my mind on a dozen other things. They could have been there for hours.''

"Or not."

"That's true. I simply can't remember."

"You have no idea how they got backstage?"

"If I knew that, I'd know who the murderer is, wouldn't I? Obviously, he—or she—saw them and decided to kill Draper with them."

He cogitated on that for an instant. "Okay, now you say you only touched the place where the blades are screwed together, when you took them out so you could turn him over."

"That's right. I was careful not to touch them anywhere else."

He exhaled a long breath. "That was quick thinking, Tess. One of the other officers dusted the shears for prints and lifted a couple from where the blades joined. Those will probably turn out to be yours. I'll need to take your prints for comparison when I come by Iris House tomorrow."

Tess nodded. "There weren't any prints on the handles?" Chief Butts would not have answered that question, but Neill didn't hesitate.

He shook his head and said, "Nope." He looked at her sharply. "That's just between you and me."

"Of course. So the murderer wiped the handles after he stabbed Draper." Tess was surprised by this revelation. She'd been imagining a burst of fury, an impulse stabbing, followed by shock and panicked retreat. But the murderer had not been too stunned by what he'd done to get rid of evidence that could tie him to the crime. It seemed the killer had had his wits about him, so maybe he hadn't struck out in blind rage, after all. The other thing that pointed to a premeditated killing was the apparent fact that the killer picked up the shears from the pew and took them backstage.

"Tell me again what Draper said before he died," Neill said.

"He said 'Nancy' and something else that sounded like 'Howard.' Then he moaned, and stopped breathing."

"You heard me ask everybody if they knew who Nancy Howard was."

Tess nodded glumly. They'd all said they didn't know any Nancy Howard. "I know it doesn't make any sense, but I'm sure about the Nancy part. I'm not so sure the last name was Howard, though. But it was something very close to that."

Neill frowned. "This pageant you all were working on today—is there a character named Nancy?"

Tess shook her head. "Maybe Draper's wife knows who Nancy is."

"If you get a chance, could you ask her when you get home? She might be more willing to talk to you than to me."

"I'll ask her," Tess said.

"And you'll let me know right away if she can tell you who Nancy Howard is?" he asked anxiously.

Tess never thought she'd wish Desmond Butts was back in town, and she couldn't imagine that she and Butts would ever be friends, but, during the investigation of a murder at last fall's Victoria Springs Quilt Show and Sale, Tess had gained a grudging respect for Butts's abilities as an investigator. Now she was beginning to wonder if Andy Neill was up to the job of catching a killer.

He met her gaze questioningly. "What?"

"Er—yes, I'll let you know if I learn anything new."

Neill shifted in the pew and leaned back, hands splayed

on his thighs. "I can't get a handle on this thing," he muttered. "Somebody at the church today killed Sherwood Draper. Okay. Lily Brookside and the deceased were giving each other the eye, which might've got Denny Brookside's back up, but Denny wouldn't kill the man for that, would he?"

"I find it hard to believe," Tess agreed.

"After all, Lily's eye gets glommed onto a lot of men. It's what she does for recreation." He glanced at Tess, a little embarrassed. "She even came on to me at a policemen's benefit last year."

Tess smiled at the thought of the bashful Neill trying to fend off Lily Brookside. "I've always assumed she's not seriously looking for a lover," she said.

"Me, too. In fact, I know a guy who tried to set up a meeting, after she'd been all over him at some shindig, but he never could pin her down to a time and place. She's a pr—well, you know what men call a woman like Lily Brookside."

Tess nodded. Indeed she did, and what Neill described was exactly how she would have expected Lily to react to a man who tried to move from flirtation to something more.

"That leaves us with only one good suspect," Neill said. "The wife."

Tess didn't miss the "us," and she understood how Neill had reached that conclusion, but in fairness she had to say, "Draper managed to make a lot of people mad today." She told him briefly about the day's events and named names, adding, "Not that I believe for one minute that Claire Chandler or Mike Tandy or Elizabeth Purcell committed murder over being squeezed out of a Christmas pageant. That's absolutely ludicrous."

Neill pondered for a moment. "So we're back to the wife."

Tess was fully aware that, in a majority of murder cases, the killer was somebody close to the victim, often the spouse or lover. But, in the brief time she'd known

Mavis Draper, the woman had gained her sympathy and pity. Tess suspected Mavis had not been happy in the marriage for some time. How *could* you be happy in a relationship where you distrusted your partner? But when rational people wanted out of a marriage, they got a divorce. Sure, divorces could get messy. But not as messy as murder.

Yet, who else but Mavis could Draper possibly have angered so deeply that she—or he—killed him?

Reluctantly, Neill got to his feet. "I want to take another look at the crime scene," he said, then added in a hopeful tone, "I'll talk to you later, after you've questioned Mrs. Draper."

Tess was getting the distinct feeling that Andy Neill expected her to perform a miracle, break down Mavis's defenses, and get a full confession. It would certainly get Neill off the hot seat. Tess hated to disappoint Neill, but she was pretty sure she would get little help from Mavis Draper.

As Tess started up the aisle, Lily Brookside burst into the sanctuary. "Officer Neill!" she said breathlessly, "I demand that you give me a bodyguard. Mavis Draper threatened to kill me!"

Neill sat Lily down in a pew and began talking to her in low tones. Tess couldn't hear what they were saying. She left the sanctuary, then felt uneasy about being alone in the foyer. She hesitated, still stunned by Lily's words. What had Mavis said or done that Lily took as a threat? Whatever it was, it must have happened backstage before Mavis, Lily, and the professor had emerged, all of them looking so strange. Perhaps she could get Neill to fill her in tomorrow when he came to Iris House.

As she crossed the foyer, her glance fell on the waste container in the corner and she remembered Bill Chandler taking a piece of paper from his pocket, unfolding it, reading it, then throwing it into the container. It was the way he'd looked at it that piqued her curiosity, as if he were surprised or confused by what was on the paper.

Tess lifted the lid and bent to peer into the container. It had been emptied recently—only a few scraps of paper lay on the bottom. Reaching in, she scooped them up in her hand. There were three visitors' cards from a rack on the back of a pew. The backs of the cards were covered with childish scribbles. Evidently a parent had used them to keep a restless child occupied during church. Then there was the litter that Tess had picked up from the floor in the sanctuary earlier. The last piece of paper looked like the one Bill Chandler had discarded. She uncrumpled it and read.

*You have twenty-four hours to do the right thing or I go to the police.*

There was no signature.

Tess read the message through three times, stunned and bewildered in equal measure. What was the "right thing"? And why would the police be interested?

She heard footsteps—probably Lily's—walking through the sanctuary toward the foyer and quickly stuffed the note into her jacket pocket.

Outside, she pulled her jacket collar up around her ears and hurried along the walk through the gathering darkness. Would she ever enter the church again without remembering Sherwood Draper, lying on the floor with those vicious-looking shears protruding from his back?

She saw the Brooksides' car still parked in a corner of the lot—Denny and the twins waiting for Lily who, at that moment, was doing her best to cause trouble for Mavis Draper. The uncharitable thought made Tess feel guilty. Maybe Lily really was afraid of Mavis.

Luke, Madison, and Curt were waiting for her in the Jeep, with the heater running and Willie Nelson's voice issuing from the tape deck, advising mamas not to let their babies grow up to be cowboys.

Luke smiled at Tess as she got in. Curt was slumped in one corner of the back seat, dozing. Madison was curled in the opposite corner, gazing out the window. She was pale and subdued and, Tess was sure, reliving the moment when she'd seen Sherwood Draper's body on the floor of the changing room.

"How you doin', Madison?" Tess asked.

Curt stirred and sat up, yawning.

"Okay," Madison said. "It's just, I keep seeing those shears sticking out of his back and all that blood." She shuddered. "It was horrible."

"I know."

"Those are the shears I used to cut the ribbon, aren't they?"

"I'm afraid so," Tess told her.

Madison's shoulders sagged.

"How about you, Curt?" Tess asked.

"I'm okay. It was a serious shock, though. I never saw a dead body before."

"I wish you kids hadn't had to see this one," Tess said.

"If only I'd left those shears in the basement," Madison said, "Professor Draper might still be alive."

"It's not your fault," Tess told her. "And 'what if's' are useless."

"Don't be hard on yourself, Madison," Luke advised.

He shifted into reverse and backed up. The Jeep's tires crunched through melting snow as they left the church. The streets were slushy, too, but the temperature was dropping. If it fell below freezing overnight, the slush would refreeze and the streets would be even more hazardous tomorrow morning than they had been today.

"What did Neill want?" Luke asked.

Tess snapped on her seat belt. "I think he's worried about how to handle the investigation in the chief's absence."

"He's not very experienced," Luke observed.

Tess murmured an agreement. "I got the feeling he needed a sounding board and I was there. He said I was observant."

"Sounds like he wants you to be his spy."

"I guess," Tess admitted, but she felt no resentment toward Neill. After all, her curiosity would spur her to look and question, regardless of Neill. "I know the people at church better than he does, and Mavis is staying with me. By the way, Neill told me to ask her to stick around a couple of days."

Curt leaned his chin over the back seat and asked eagerly, "Does he think Mrs. Draper killed her husband?"

"I'm not sure he has any firm opinion about who did it, not yet," Tess said judiciously. She would keep Lily's accusation to herself for now. "He just wants to talk to Mrs. Draper before she leaves."

Curt sat back in his seat. "I'll bet he thinks she did it."

"You don't know anything about it," Madison muttered. "I don't think Mrs. Draper killed the professor. Do you, Tess?"

"I don't know what to think, honey." But when she reflected upon it, Tess came up against the same wall as Neill. Nobody else at the church today had a past history with Sherwood Draper, not a history that hid a motive for murder.

Unless something major happened between Draper and one or both of the Brooksides last year in Vail, something that had festered in Denny or Lily for a year and drove them to murder when Draper turned up in Victoria Springs. And Lily *had* been the cause for Draper's being brought there. Could she have had a far more sinister motive than a little light flirtation? Accusing Mavis could be her way of taking the spotlight off herself.

Impossible, Tess told herself. She'd known the Brooksides since she moved to Victoria Springs and had never suspected that either was capable of committing murder.

As for Claire Chandler and Mike Tandy, they were both indignant at having an outsider running the show and angry over Draper's high-handedness, but they'd been dealing with it in their own unique ways—Claire by throwing herself into putting on a children's program that would overshadow Draper's pageant and, in her spare time, disrupting Draper's schedule whenever she could, and Mike by showing up in that Santa suit to tweak his nose at Draper and more or less ignoring the professor otherwise.

Elizabeth Purcell had been outraged by Draper's updated pageant and the taped music, but Tess's mind boggled at the idea of the seventy-year-old ex–school teacher as a killer. Elizabeth, as organist, had been shut out of Draper's pageant, but there would be other days and other programs.

Bill Chandler and Blanche Tandy weren't even on Tess's tentative and extremely shaky suspect list. Both had been worried about their spouses' reactions to Draper, but they'd had no conflict with the professor themselves. Besides, Tess knew both Bill and Blanche, and could not picture either of them turning violent. But then, as she fingered the note in her pocket, Tess wondered how well she knew Bill Chandler, after all.

As for the others who'd been at the church when Sherwood was killed, in Tess's mind they were peripheral at best.

And the teenagers? They'd been intent on each other and decorating the fellowship hall. Tess didn't think any of them had given more than a passing thought to Sherwood Draper.

She was jolted out of her reverie by the Jeep coming to a stop. While she had mentally checked off suspects, they'd reached Iris House. "Want to come in for a while?" she asked Luke.

"Can't. I need to get Sidney's Jeep back to him and do some work before the market opens tomorrow." Aware of the two pairs of eyes observing them from the back seat, he gave Tess a chaste peck on the cheek. "Call me in the morning if the roads are slick and you need to go somewhere."

Tess, Madison, and Curt crunched up the front walk and stomped mud and snow off their boots on the porch mat before going inside. The house was dim and quiet. In the foyer, Tess peered up the stairs, wondering if Mavis was resting. Or was the poor woman up there, desolated, grieving alone—maybe even in shock?

Tess dug out the key to her apartment door and handed it to Madison.

"I'm starved," Curt said. "What's for dinner?"

Tess had taken a package of ground beef from the freezer that morning. "How does a hamburger and fries sound?" She'd better feed them first. She'd check on Mavis a little later.

"Great. Two burgers sounds even better."

Madison got the door open. Curt and Tess followed her into the apartment. "I'll bet Daddy didn't warn you, Tess," Madison said over her shoulder. "Curt's *always* hungry."

"Yeah, but I'm not picky," Curt said.

"That's true," Madison agreed. "You'll eat anything—as long as it doesn't move and has ketchup on it."

Tess closed the door behind her. "That's good, because I'm not the world's best cook—that title belongs to Gertie Bogart."

Curt smacked his lips, shrugged off his jacket, and tossed it on Tess's couch. "She promised she'd make Belgian waffles tomorrow morning," he said as he headed down the hall toward the kitchen. "With strawberries and whipped cream."

Madison looked at Tess. "Hog heaven," she said. Most of her normal color had returned. Tess thought Madison and Curt would be okay, but she'd remain watchful. There were a couple of good psychologists in Victoria Springs, either of whom could provide professional counseling if Madison or Curt seemed to need it.

Primrose wandered in from Tess's bedroom to weave between Tess's legs. She bent down to stroke the Persian's soft fur and heard Curt open the refrigerator door. "You got any ice cream, Tess?"

"Chocolate chip and butter pecan," Tess called, "but wait till after we have dinner."

The refrigerator door thumped shut, and she heard cabinet doors opening and closing. "Okay. I found some cookies to snack on."

Tess and Madison looked at each other again and, suddenly, they both started laughing. And couldn't stop. Partly, it was semi-hysteria, a delayed reaction to the horrible scene they'd stumbled on at the church.

Finally, they collapsed on the couch in a heap, hugging each other. Primrose watched them disdainfully and left the room. After a moment, Madison took a deep breath and wiped her eyes. "We're awful, to be laughing at a time like this."

"No, it's okay," Tess said. "I'm glad you can laugh about something."

Madison shrugged out of her jacket. "I know I've been kind of a pain since we got here."

"I understand you didn't want to come to Victoria Springs and miss some of your friends' parties."

She made a face. "Big mouth told you."

"I mentioned that you didn't seem happy, and Curt told me why you weren't, that's all."

"I'm sorry I wouldn't talk to you when you picked us up at the airport yesterday."

"I assumed you were tired."

Madison stood and reached for her jacket. "It didn't have anything to do with you, Tess."

Tess pushed herself off the couch and started toward the kitchen. "I know."

Madison hugged her jacket to her chest. "Not much, anyway."

Tess halted in her tracks and turned around. "What?"

Madison gave her a weak smile. "It's only—well, sometimes I get kind of tired of having you thrown up to me."

Tess gaped at her. "What on earth are you talking about?"

"Daddy's always telling me what a good student you were, what a success you're making of Iris House, how proud he is of you."

Tess was speechless for the longest moment. Even though Tess had been in her last year at the university when her father and the rest of the family left the country, she'd felt abandoned. For a while, she'd wallowed in self-pity, telling herself that her father had a new family and no longer loved her as much as he loved his other children. She'd actually been jealous of Madison and Curt because they were with her father and she wasn't.

Finally, she said, "I didn't know that, Madison. I'm sorry."

"Forget it," Madison said grandly. "It's not your fault that you're better at everything than I am."

Tess could hardly believe her ears. This was Madison talking, the girl she'd thought so self-confident. "That's not true, and you know it," she protested. "Your teachers say you have acting ability. Why I couldn't act my way out of a paper bag."

"Well, I do enjoy acting—usually. But the Christmas pageant is ruined for me now."

"Claire will take over and probably throw out the professor's pageant and come up with something totally different. Just tell her you don't want to be involved in it."

"Can I?"

"Of course you can."

She beamed. "Good. That's a relief. And I really don't care that Daddy thinks you're a better daughter than I am."

"He thinks no such thing!" Tess protested. "He probably means to motivate you by comparing us." And he should know better, Tess thought. She'd have a word with her father when he got there. "You want to know a secret?"

Madison nodded.

"I've been envious ever since you arrived because you're so pretty, like Aunt Dahlia."

Madison blushed. "I'm not really."

"Of course you are. Boyd Brookside certainly noticed."

"Boyd's nice." She smiled dreamily, then added hastily, "Brenda and Eddie, too."

"We'll get you something to wear to the sock hop," Tess said as Madison headed for her room. She thought she could work in a shopping trip sometime tomorrow.

"Don't worry about it," Madison said offhandedly, as if she hadn't insisted only hours ago that she needed to shop for something dressy. "This morning I happened to look in your closet and saw a beautiful red sweater. Maybe I could borrow that?"

Happened to? Tess thought, and suppressed a smile at the idea of Madison examining her wardrobe. Curiosity seemed to run in the family. "Of course," she said. "Do you have something to wear it with?"

"Brenda says all the kids will wear jeans."

Silently blessing Brenda, Tess went to the kitchen, where Curt sat at the table with a big glass of milk and a now-empty cookie sack.

# Chapter 11

Bill Chandler sat at his kitchen table, drinking re-heated coffee left from the breakfast pot. Watching him remove the cup from the microwave, Claire had shuddered and said she didn't know how he drank that warmed-over sludge. The fact was, it hardly mattered how the coffee tasted. He was too absorbed in his troubled thoughts to notice.

Claire was talking, but he'd tuned her out. Claire was always rattling on about something. He was used to it and normally it didn't bother him. But tonight he wished she'd shut up long enough for him to think.

Claire stood at the range, turning catfish fillets in a sizzling frying pan. "—so who do you think it was?" When he didn't respond, she looked over her shoulder at him. "Bill, I'm talking to you."

Would it kill her to keep her mouth closed for ten minutes? He glanced up at her. "What?"

"Good heavens, do you need your hearing checked?"

"There's nothing wrong with my hearing." This was one of the times when he wished there were.

Her middle-aged face sagged, but her eyes were alert. "Then where were you?"

"I'm tired, Claire."

She gave an offended little sniff. "So am I, but

you don't see me sitting on my butt. I have to cook dinner."

And whose fault was it that she was tired? He'd tried to get her to stay home today, but no, she had to stick her nose in the mess at church and—oh, hell, if only she'd listened to him. He stared morosely at the coffee in the bottom of his cup.

She set the lid on the frying pan and turned around. "I was talking about Sherwood Draper," she prattled on, "and who killed him. It has to be either Mavis Draper or Denny Brookside."

"Why?"

"Why what?" she asked irritably.

"Why does it have to be Mrs. Draper or Denny?"

"My God, you really didn't hear a word I said."

"You want an apology?" he grunted.

Claire looked at him speculatively. "What I want is to have a little conversation with my husband. As I was saying, the murderer is obviously Mavis or Denny because of what happened backstage earlier."

"And what was that?"

"Well, I can't give you all the tawdry little details since I wasn't there, but obviously Mavis and Denny caught Lily and the professor, if not actually *doing* it, then in the preliminary stages, so to speak."

Bill took a swallow of coffee and, for the first time, noticed how bitter it was. He made a face and set the cup down. "Doing it? If you mean Lily and Draper were having sex, for God's sake why don't you say that, Claire."

Her brows drew together in a tight frown and she planted her hands on her hips. "Okay. They were having sex, or working up to it. Is that better?" He didn't bother responding, which didn't derail his wife. "You've been acting weird ever since we got back from the church. If you're not ignoring me completely, you're snapping my head off. What is *wrong* with you?"

His eyes lingered on her for a moment, and then he

sighed heavily. "We've been questioned in a murder investigation, Claire."

"Oh, good grief! Everybody at the church today was questioned—or will be. It doesn't mean anything."

"Whatever you say, Claire."

Uneasiness flickered in her green eyes. "Don't tell me you didn't see them—Denny and Mavis, I mean—when they came back onstage after they caught their spouses in a compromising position."

"You don't know that's what happened."

"What else could it be? Their faces looked like stone. Stiff. You could have struck a match off either one of them. I tell you, they're the only ones who had a motive."

"Some people might think *you* did. You made it pretty clear what you thought of Draper and of Pastor Matt, for bringing him here."

"Why, that's—" she sputtered. "That's too ridiculous for words. Do you actually think I'd kill someone over a Christmas pageant?"

"I didn't say that's what I think. I'm saying what it might look like to other people." His chair scraped back as he stood abruptly. "I need your keys."

"What?"

"The church keys. I have to go back."

Claire's prying eyes appraised him. "What for?"

"I left my new gloves there."

"Dinner's almost ready. The gloves will be there tomorrow."

He raised his voice. "The keys, Claire. Are they in your purse?"

She gaped at him. "Yes, but—"

He walked out in the middle of her protest, found her purse in their bedroom, emptied its contents on the bed, and fished around until he pulled out the church keys. He brushed past Claire, who'd followed him to the bedroom door, and left the house without a word.

\* \* \*

Claire, who for once was astounded into silence by her husband's mysterious behavior, walked to the bed and began throwing wallet, lipstick, comb, compact, tissues, and several ballpoint pens back into her purse. As she set the purse on the dresser, she saw Bill's gloves lying right there in plain sight. Where he'd left them.

"Bill!" She ran to the door, wrenched it open, and saw the car's taillights disappearing around the corner at the end of the block.

Dinner was sandwiches made from leftover meat loaf and hot chocolate. They'd eaten in strained silence and then the twins had gone to the basement rec room where they'd turned on the stereo. Lily could feel the bass beat through the kitchen floor. Denny was in the den now, in his easy chair, his feet up on the ottoman.

Having cleared the table and put the dirty dishes in the dishwasher, Lily looked around the kitchen for something else to do. Everything was in its place, the room spotless. For an instant, the gay Christmas decorations so lovingly placed there seemed to mock her.

Nothing to do but join her husband in the den.

Lily had been dreading this moment, but she couldn't keep her anxiety to herself any longer.

A book lay open on Denny's lap, but he wasn't reading. He was staring into the fire. Lily walked to the fireplace and made a show of warming her hands, but she felt his gaze on her back and it made her uncomfortable. She sat down on the couch.

Denny picked up his book and pretended to read.

Lily watched him, wondering what he was thinking. Who was this man whose bed she'd shared for more than twenty years, this man she'd thought she knew so well? "Did you see anybody backstage?" she asked.

It was a moment before he looked at her. In the silence the fire popped, sending upward a spray of orange coals. "When?"

"I saw you go back there while the choir was on its

break." This was the reason she'd made such a fuss about Mavis to Officer Neill. She'd wanted to protect Denny—if he needed protecting. When Mavis caught her and Sherwood in the dressing room, Mavis had said she could kill the both of them. Lily hadn't taken her words literally. Even after Sherwood's body was found, Lily hadn't remembered Mavis's words until she was in the car with her family, still worrying about Denny's behavior. And she'd made him wait while she went back to tell Neill.

He looked at her stonily for a moment, then glanced back at his book. "No. I didn't see anyone backstage."

But shortly before that Lily had seen Sherwood go backstage. Denny could hardly have missed him. He was lying. Fear clutched Lily's heart. She wanted Mavis to be the killer, but she couldn't be sure.

She watched Denny until it became clear that he intended to say no more. Finally, she cleared her throat and said, "Nothing happened between Sherwood and me."

He slammed the book closed and threw it on the floor. "Nothing? Is that what you call it?"

So he knew she'd kissed Sherwood. Of course, he knew, but she had been so hoping . . .

"Yes, I call it that because it was meaningless."

He gazed at the fire, his hands clenching the arms of his chair, his jaw working.

"I didn't mean for it to happen, Denny," she said in a small, pleading voice.

Angrily, he kicked aside the ottoman and stood. He hitched up his trousers over his stomach. "Give me a break, Lily! You let him know what you wanted, and he obliged you."

"That's not true," she wailed. "He took me by surprise."

He laughed mirthlessly. "That's rich, Lily. You're the biggest flirt in town. What do you expect?"

"You know I don't mean anything by it. I—"

"Shut up, Lily, and listen to me for a minute. I'm sick

of hearing that you don't mean what your actions so clearly say you do.''

"Denny—"

"Shut up, I said! It will never happen again, Lily. Understand?''

"How dare—''

He raised his voice to drown out her words. "From now on you will keep your hands and your suggestive looks and secret smiles to yourself. You will not flirt with other men. I've had it up to here, and I won't tolerate it any longer. Is that clear?''

Tears sprang to her eyes and she rose from the sofa, trembling with outrage. He had never talked to her like this before. "You don't give me orders, Denny Brookside!''

"Call it whatever you want. Call it a request, if that makes it easier to swallow. But you change your ways!''

"Or what?'' she demanded.

"Or get out!''

She sucked in a shocked breath as he stalked from the room.

"I will not get out! This is my home!'' She ran after him into the hall. "I know you had words with Sherwood backstage, Denny. Did it get out of hand? What *happened*? You have to talk to me, Denny.''

He uttered a furious curse. "Stay away from me, Lily, or I won't be responsible for what I do.''

"Like you aren't responsible for what happened to Sherwood?'' she shrieked.

He went into their bedroom and slammed the door in her face.

"Mom?''

Lily almost jumped out of her skin. Boyd stood in the hall behind her, his face pinched and pale. How much of the argument had he heard? "Don't sneak up on people like that, Boyd.''

"I'm sorry. I didn't mean to scare you, but I've got a problem.''

Great. Join the club. Lily calmed herself with difficulty. "What is it, dear?"

"Today at the church, I saw something and I don't know what to do about it."

He let himself in a side door. The interior of the church at night was a black world of silence so thick it seemed to gather, pulsing and pressing, all around him, like some huge amoebic creature, alive, breathing. He smelled lemon oil and floor wax. As he fumbled for a light switch, a dull noise sounded deep in the bowels of the church.

He drew his breath in sharply, and the next instant let it out slowly as he realized he'd heard the furnace turning itself on in the basement.

One more sweep of his hand across the wall and he touched the switch and flipped it up. The amoebic creature retreated as pale light revealed the hallway bordered on both sides by classroom doors. He hurried along the hall, not wanting to spend any more time than necessary in the building. He switched on another light next to the foyer entrance. Pushing through the door, he flipped yet another switch and cast one uneasy glance toward the sanctuary, seeing only blackness behind the glass pane.

He stood still for a moment, listening, still a little edgy with the weight of the silence. Then he walked quickly to the waste container in the corner, removed the cover, and peered down at a few scraps of paper. Upending the container, he emptied the contents on the foyer floor. It took but a minute to pick up each piece, look at it, and discard it, another minute to go through the scraps a second time.

The note wasn't there.

His heart lurched with alarm as he tried to think what that meant. He felt his stomach tighten. Why had he thrown the note away?

When he'd found it in his overcoat pocket, he'd been baffled by the message. He was sure it hadn't been there when he arrived at the church and hung his coat on a hook. And it had made no sense—then. A practical joke, he'd thought. Those teenagers. Probably didn't even know whose coat they'd put it in.

Stupid, stupid!

Only later, after he'd had time to think about it, had he understood the sinister message.

And now it was gone.

Bill Chandler, community leader, trusted insurance provider, noted for his common sense and general unflappability, felt a stirring of panic. Okay, now, stay calm, he told himself. Nothing to worry about. The janitor had made his rounds that evening. He must have emptied the trash in one of the big bins in the alley out back. The note was lost in a barrel full of litter. Somebody, Pastor Matt, probably must have come through the foyer afterward and dropped in the litter that was in the container now.

Unless . . .

Oh, God, no! What if the police had found that note?

Dinner at the Tandy house was consumed, or rather picked at, in heavy silence. Blanche was bursting to talk to Mike about what had happened at church, but she didn't want to do it in Eddie's presence. Poor Eddie kept looking worriedly from Mike to Blanche and hardly touched his food. Finally, he asked to be excused.

"You haven't eaten two bites," Blanche said.

"I'm not hungry."

"All right then." She could hardly urge him to eat when she had no interest in food herself.

Eddie left the table. When Blanche heard his bedroom door close, she said, "I keep thinking that man might not have died if—"

Startled, Mike glanced at her. "What?"

"If you and Claire hadn't made such a to-do over the pageant, maybe Professor Draper would still be alive."

"Are you accusing me and Claire of killing him?"

"No, of course not. But I never saw you treat anybody the way you treated the professor—with such rudeness.

You certainly contributed to the heated situation at church.''

''What about Elizabeth? And the others who spoke out at the meeting?'

''Them, too. But you and Claire were the worst. Mike, you know that's true.''

Scowling, Mike shoved back his chair, his own dinner barely half-eaten. ''It's always nice to know your loyal wife is in your corner,'' he muttered indignantly.

''Mike, I only meant to say—''

He held up a hand. ''You've said enough already, Blanche.'' He rose and stalked away from the table, toward the door leading to the living room.

Blanche caught a movement from the corner of her eye and, turning, saw Eddie hovering in the other doorway, the one leading to the hallway and bedrooms.

''What do you want, Eddie?'' she asked tightly.

At the sound of the irritation in her voice, Mike hesitated in the other doorway. It was probably the first time since Eddie had come to stay with them that she'd shown any impatience with the boy.

Blanche already regretted her sharpness. ''I didn't mean to snap at you, Eddie.''

''That's okay. Mike, where are you going?''

''For a drive,'' Mike said and continued through the living room to the foyer closet where he'd left his coat.

Eddie went after him. ''Could I come with you?''

''No,'' Mike said curtly.

''We could talk.''

''I said no.''

''But Mike—''

''Not now, Eddie!'' Mike snapped, his voice rising. A moment later, Blanche heard the front door close behind him.

Returning to the kitchen, Eddie looked absolutely crushed by Mike's rebuff.

''He's just upset because of what happened at church,

Eddie," Blanche said. "We all are. It has nothing to do with you."

Eddie went back to his room without another word.

Blanche continued to sit at the table, her head in her hands. She'd only wanted to talk about the murder, to try to understand what had happened and who might be responsible, but she'd said it all wrong and Mike's feelings were hurt. Well, she'd try to talk to him about it later. More importantly, she'd insist that Mike apologize for yelling at Eddie, who could tolerate abuse from anybody but his idol.

Tess tapped on the door of the Darcy Flame Suite.

"Who is it?" She sounded immeasurably weary.

"It's Tess, Mavis. May I come in?"

It was a few moments before she opened the door. She had on a navy velour robe with a lace collar. Her face without makeup was almost as white as the collar, and behind her glasses, the whites around the pale blue irises were streaked with red.

Tess stepped inside and quietly closed the door behind her. "Is there anything I can do for you, Mavis?"

She walked away from the door with great caution, like a much older woman, and sank into an ivory slipper chair. The pale fabric made her look even more washed out. "Thank you, but no. There's nothing anyone can do."

"Have you been able to rest at all?"

Mavis shook her head, flopping a springy blond curl onto her forehead. She raked it back with her fingers. "I've been thinking about funeral arrangements. I can't begin to get over this until all that's behind me."

Tess sat in the other slipper chair. "I'm sure it won't be too long before they release the body."

She looked up with a puzzled frown. "Release? You mean they might keep him a while? Why would they do that?'

"Well—" Tess hesitated, not wanting to say the words, but apparently the obvious reason for a delay in releasing the body hadn't occurred to Mavis. "There's the autopsy . . ."

"Autopsy!" Mavis seemed appalled by the idea.

"They always do an autopsy in cases of unnatural death," Tess said gently.

Mavis looked a little frightened then and, removing her glasses, she dropped them in her lap and covered her face with her hands. Tess watched her, at a loss for words. When Mavis looked up, she appeared troubled but resigned. "I hadn't thought about that—because, well, it's obvious what he died of . . ."

"It's the law," Tess said.

"Oh." She leaned back in the chair and plucked at a strip of coral piping. She looked naked and more vulnerable without her glasses. "I'll go home tomorrow then. I can, at least, make the arrangements."

"Officer Neill asked me to give you a message. He wants you to stay here for a couple of days."

Her expression reflected both anger and apprehension as they fought for the upper hand. "I'll go crazy here with nothing to do but stare at four walls." Her tone was defensive. "You could have forgotten to tell me," she added hopefully. "I don't have to stay if I don't want to, do I?"

"I think it would be wise," Tess said carefully, "to cooperate with the police."

Her lips trembled. "Are you saying . . . ? Oh, dear God, are they going to arrest me?"

Tess reached across the space between them to touch Mavis's hand. It was cold. "They only want to ask you a few questions. Officer Neill said he'd be here between eight and ten tomorrow morning. I'm sure it's simply routine." For now, she added to herself. Andy Neill didn't have the evidence to detain anybody at this point, unless Lily Brookside really hadn't exaggerated something Mavis had said.

But why had Mavis jumped to the conclusion that she was about to be arrested?

"You shouldn't be alone here, Mavis. Isn't there someone I can call for you?"

Her hand tightened on the arm of her chair. "No. I already phoned my mother in Boston. She'll come down and stay with me for a few days when I get back home."

"That's good. You'll need someone."

"She insisted on coming. My mother and I never got along." Her voice shook. "She didn't want me to marry Sherwood. She said we'd live in poverty and he'd end up breaking my heart."

Tess wasn't sure how to respond to that. "That must've been a long time ago," she said finally. "I'm sure she's forgotten all about it."

She laughed mirthlessly. "You don't know my mother. I'd never tell her, but she was right. Not about the poverty. We lived comfortably enough. I never needed a lot of material things. But Mother was right about the other."

Having already sensed that Mavis wasn't happy in her marriage, Tess said simply, "I'm sorry, Mavis."

She gave a helpless little shrug. Tess watched her distractedly finger the chair's piping again, wondering if she should leave the woman to her sad thoughts until tomorrow. But Neill might phone her tonight, if she didn't phone him, and Tess didn't think it would be any easier to question Mavis tomorrow.

Mavis was staring at the carpet in a nearsighted, unfocused way that meant she wasn't really seeing it.

"Who is Nancy Howard?" Tess asked.

Mavis blinked and glanced up. "Who?"

"Nancy Howard."

She looked blank. "I never heard of her. Why?"

Tess had gone this far, she had to finish it, get it over with. "Professor Draper said the name before—before he died. At least I think that's what he said. I know he said Nancy something, and it sounded like Howard."

Mavis's brow furrowed. "Is that what he said? I—I was outside the room. I didn't understand." She took a deep, trembly breath. "His sister's name was Nancy, but he couldn't have meant her. Nancy Howard doesn't sound anything like Nancy Draper."

Tess remembered now that Draper had looked toward the changing room doorway, where Madison stood, when he said those words. "Is that the sister Madison reminded him of?"

She nodded. "Sherwood had only one sister."

"And she isn't married?"

"Wasn't," Mavis said. "Nancy was killed in a car wreck—let's see, it must be almost twenty years ago now. She was only eighteen, a freshman at the University of Maine—that's where it happened. The driver was drunk. Sherwood and I had just announced our engagement. It should have been a joyful time . . ." She lifted her hand impotently, then let it drop back to the chair arm. "Nancy's death changed everything. Sherwood's mother never got over it. She died two years afterward, grieved herself to death. Sherwood's father lived for several more years, but he withdrew into himself, became housebound. Nancy was a change-of-life baby and the whole family doted on her."

"What a tragedy," Tess murmured.

Mavis sighed an agreement and laid her head against the back of her chair, exhausted by the other, more immediate tragedy. "I couldn't see it then, but there was a cloud over my marriage from the start."

"Because of Nancy's death?" Tess asked.

"Yes. Sherwood was so torn up over her death. I saw that as evidence of how deeply he was capable of loving. I was so naive, so dazzled by him. But I didn't know my husband as well as I thought." She paused, then added musingly, "Perhaps no woman ever does. Some are just lucky."

Tess was thinking, Nancy Draper—Nancy Howard. It was true, they didn't sound anything alike. "And you're sure you never heard of a Nancy Howard?" she asked.

"I'm sure," Mavis said and closed her eyes. "You know, Tess, it's ironic that he died today."

"What do you mean?"

She opened her eyes, squinted at Tess. "Today I found Sherwood kissing Lily Brookside in the changing room—the very room where—where he died."

"Mavis . . ."

"Oh, it wasn't the first time. But I knew it had to be the last. I decided to end my miserable marriage."

For a couple of heartbeats, Tess was sure Mavis was about to confess to murder. And wouldn't that take a load off Andy Neill? But then, she said, "I made up my mind to divorce Sherwood."

Tess wondered if Mavis would tell Andy Neill about finding her husband and Lily Brookside together. But Lily probably already had. "What did you say when you found them?" Tess asked.

Mavis looked bewildered. "Say? I don't remember. No telling. I was so angry."

"Did you threaten Lily?"

She raked a hand through her hair. "Is that what she said? Well, I might have said something about wanting to kill them both. I didn't mean it, of course. As I said, I'd made up my mind to get a divorce. Lily Brookside was welcome to him." Her voice broke a little, but she recovered quickly. "Now it's been taken out of my hands."

Was that a convenient coincidence, from Mavis's point of view? Tess wondered. Or a tragic one?

Mavis laid her head back again, closed her eyes, and murmured, "I'm so very tired."

It was clearly a dismissal. Tess stood, hesitated. She hated leaving the woman alone like this, but that seemed to be what Mavis wanted. "I'm going downstairs now. Could I bring you up some dinner?"

She shook her head. "I couldn't eat."

"All right then." Tess paused at the door. "If you change your mind, or need anything else, just pick up the phone and call me. My number's in that little book beside the phone."

Mavis didn't respond, and Tess let herself out.

*Chapter 12*

"Whew! That street up the hill is a sheet of glass," Andy Neill exclaimed the next morning as Tess admitted him to Iris House. She had already listened to the report of school closings. Victoria Springs students had another day off and Tess had phoned Gertie to tell her not to risk getting out. Using Gertie's recipe, she made Belgian waffles for Madison and Curt's breakfast and took a tray up to Mavis.

Boyd Brookside had called to say he and Brenda were leaving the house on foot with the sleds and would meet Madison and Curt at the top of the hill a block from Iris House. Madison and Curt had bundled up and left the house five minutes ago.

"Don't drive if you don't have to, Tess," Neill advised.

"I don't plan to until later this afternoon," Tess told him. According to the TV weatherman, the temperature should rise to forty by noon and the ice and snow would melt quickly. After lunch, she'd take Curt and Madison to pick out a Christmas tree.

"I brought the fingerprint kit," Neill said.

Tess led him into the parlor, where he opened the kit and directed her to press her fingers against the inked pad and then carefully transfer the prints to a sheet of paper. He labeled each print for comparison with the ones found on the murder weapon. When he'd finished, Tess said, "Before you speak to Mrs. Draper, there's something I need to talk to you about."

Stuffing the kit back into its leather carrying case, he looked at her expectantly.

"It's about Lily's accusation."

"That Mavis Draper might try to kill her?"

Tess nodded. "It's very possible that Lily is exaggerating something Mavis said when she caught her husband kissing Lily Brookside yesterday afternoon in the changing room."

"The room where her husband was killed?"

Tess nodded again. "Yes. Mavis admits that she said something about wanting to kill them both. But she says she didn't mean it literally."

He cocked his head. "What else would you expect her to say?"

"Andy," Tess said earnestly, "I don't think it's the first time Professor Draper was involved with another woman. Apparently, it was just the last straw for his wife."

He nodded sagely. "So she killed him."

"I'm not at all sure she did, no matter what Lily thinks. I mean, why this time, if he had a history of that kind of thing?"

"Like you said, this time was the last straw. She blew. Couldn't take it anymore."

"Maybe, but Mrs. Draper told me she intended to get a divorce, that it was ironic he died when he did."

"Ironic, huh?" he snorted and pulled a folded piece of paper from his pocket. "I've got an arrest warrant right here. Wasn't sure I would serve it today, but I just changed my mind."

"I hope it wasn't anything I said—" How had he gotten an arrest warrant so quickly? "Mavis was shocked and angry when she caught Lily and her husband kissing, and she blurted out something about wanting to kill them both. People say things like that in anger all the time."

"But the people they say it to don't generally turn up dead the same day."

There was that. "Surely, Andy, that's not enough to arrest Mavis for murder!"

"She had a strong motive, Tess."

"But I still can't believe a judge would issue a warrant based on what amounts to hearsay."

He interrupted her protest. "You're right, I couldn't have gotten a warrant based on that alone. I got a phone call early this morning from Lily Brookside."

Lily again?

"Mrs. Draper picked up those shears from the front pew and took them backstage. She was seen."

"By Lily?" Personally, Tess would take whatever Lily said against Mavis with a large grain of salt.

He shook his head. "Her son, Boyd. He finally told his mother and she called me. I want you to keep that under your hat, Tess."

"Of course."

"Which room is she in?" Neill asked.

She could see it would be futile to ask him to delay the arrest another day or two. The evidence was circumstantial, but it looked very bad for Mavis Draper. "The Darcy Flame Suite at the end of the upstairs hall."

Tess waited anxiously in the foyer until Andy Neill brought Mavis Draper downstairs a few minutes later. Mavis's makeup had been applied with a hasty and too generous hand. She looked like a corpse prepared by an incompetent funeral director. Tess was relieved to see that Neill hadn't thought it necessary to handcuff her. "Mavis, I'm so sorry. Is there anything I can I do to help?"

"Do you know a good lawyer?" Her voice was dull, toneless, as if she'd resigned herself to what was happening.

Tess could think of only one name. "Try Cody Yount. He's young but good in the courtroom, I hear. If Cody can't take your case, he'll recommend someone."

Neill opened the door and preceded Mavis outside. She

looked back at Tess. "I swear on everything I hold dear that I didn't kill Sherwood, Tess." Her voice shook and her eyes held Tess's in a clear call for help.

Tess returned to her apartment, thinking that Andy Neill had been too eager to make an arrest.

All at once, she remembered the note Bill Chandler had received and she knew she should have told Neill about it.

She went to her closet, dug the note out of her jacket pocket, and read it again.

*You have twenty-four hours to do the right thing or I go to the police.*

It sounded sinister, but she wasn't at all sure it was connected to Sherwood Draper's murder. If only she knew who'd left the note in Bill's coat.

She phoned Blanche Tandy to give her the news of Mavis Draper's arrest. "That was fast," Blanche said.

Tess voiced her reservations. "Maybe too fast. The evidence is pretty thin, from what I know, and Mavis says she didn't do it."

"What would you expect her to say?"

That's what Neill had asked, and no wonder. Many hardened criminals proclaimed their innocence to the end. But Tess was having a difficult time seeing Mavis Draper as a criminal, hardened or otherwise. For one thing Sherwood Draper's last words continued to bother her.

"It just doesn't feel right to me, Blanche." If you were dying, wouldn't you name your murderer with your last breath? Especially after Tess had asked the professor the direct question. Yet Draper's final words had been Nancy and something like Howard. There was no Nancy at the church yesterday, but Tess remained convinced the name had something to do with Draper's murder.

But did it have anything to do with the note Bill Chandler had discarded? "I found something in the church foyer yesterday, Blanche. I think it was left there during the choir's break.''

"What was it?"

"I'd rather not say at this point, but I was wondering if you noticed anybody shuffling through the coats on the hooks near the door to the classroom wing.''

"Most of that time I was in the closet going through the choir's robes to see which ones needed repairs or cleaning. I saw Draper pacing through the foyer a couple of times, but then I closed the door and I couldn't see the foyer after that.''

"Did Draper see you?"

"I don't think so. From the glimpses I had of him, he seemed preoccupied. I do remember that, after I'd closed the door, I heard him again, recognized his footsteps, and I think he stopped pacing for several moments before he went back into the sanctuary. But, as I said, I couldn't see him. I guess he could have put something in his coat then. Was it his pipe?''

"I can't tell you any more right now, Blanche," Tess repeated.

"No, it couldn't have been his pipe," Blanche mused. "It must be something—well, odd, or you wouldn't be asking me about it. Does it have anything to do with the murder?''

"I don't know, Blanche." But she intended to find out. "Did you notice anybody else in the foyer during that time?''

"Several people. I can't say who because I didn't see them. But several times I heard footsteps that didn't sound like Draper's. I'd guess that a number of people passed through the foyer while I was in the closet.''

"You don't remember any of them stopping long enough to put something in a coat pocket?''

Blanche gave it some thought. "I don't know. I wasn't paying that much attention, Tess.''

"Well, that's certainly reasonable," Tess said. "Thanks for your help, Blanche. Talk to you later.''

"Tess—?"

Tess hung up before Blanche could ask any more questions and looked at the words of the mysterious message again. How could she find out if they were written by Sherwood Draper?

The answer was obvious. She went to the window and looked out. Later in the day, if the streets were clear, she'd pay a visit to the jail.

Mavis looked terribly small and defenseless in the green coveralls worn by all the prisoners. She'd been crying. Her eyes were swollen, her nose shiny and red.

Curt had wanted to come into the visitor's room with Tess. "I never visited anybody in jail before, Tess," he'd said.

"I should hope not," she'd retorted and told him to wait for her with Madison in what passed for the police station's reception room, a cramped area with brown tile floor and walls covered with wanted posters. An officer sat behind the counter that separated the small space into two smaller spaces. As she left, she heard Curt asking the officer how many murderers they'd had in their jail.

The visitor's room doubled as the booking room and visitors were separated from prisoners by a glass partition with a speaker embedded in it. A female officer had brought Mavis into the room behind the glass, led her to a chair, then walked to the closed door, folded her arms, and waited.

Tess stepped close to the speaker which was level with Mavis's throat. "How are you?" she asked.

Pain and desperation flooded Mavis's pale face. "I've had better days. I've had better *years*."

Visitors were only allowed fifteen minutes, so Tess got right to the point. "Mavis, they'll only let me stay a few minutes. If I'm to help you, I have to ask some questions."

"Go ahead."

"Somebody saw you take those shears backstage. Why did you do that?"

"If I didn't kill Sherwood, you mean?" She glanced behind her anxiously, then hissed, "I'd give anything if I hadn't touched the damned things, Tess. I don't know why I picked them up. After I saw Sherwood and Lily embracing—I—I came back into the sanctuary. But, watching them up on the stage made me sick, so I went into one of the changing rooms to compose myself." Deep frown lines ridged her forehead. "I didn't even realize I was holding the shears until I looked in the mirror and saw them. I'd forgotten I'd picked them up, and it scared me. I just threw them down, and that's the last I saw of them."

Oh, dear. It didn't sound at all good for Mavis. If she could forget picking up the shears, perhaps she could forget killing her husband. At least, that's how Andy Neill would respond to her explanation.

"Did you get hold of Cody Yount?"

She nodded. "He came right over. Said he'd take my case and told me not to speak to anybody else about it. I—I shouldn't even be talking to you."

"Then we won't talk about the case," Tess said. She glanced at the waiting officer and saw she'd moved to a window and was looking out. Hastily, she took the note from her pocket and pressed it up against the glass, down low where Mavis's body obstructed the female officer's view, should she turn around. "Do you recognize this handwriting?" she whispered.

Mavis bent forward and adjusted her glasses on her nose with one finger. "That's Sherwood's writing." She looked at Tess, nonplussed. "Where did you get that?"

"I—er, found it. Have you ever seen this note before?"

She shook her head. "What does it mean?"

Tess put the note back in her pocket. "I have no idea. I thought you might."

"Well, I don't." She frowned thoughtfully. "Could it have been a joke?"

"Was your husband in the habit of playing that kind of joke on other people?"

"No, he wasn't. Sherwood didn't have much of a sense of humor. That note sounds like a threat, Tess." She looked at Tess sharply. "Sherwood didn't know anybody in Victoria Springs except the Brooksides. He must have sent it to one of them. But why would he threaten to go to the police?"

If Tess knew that, she'd know what to do about the note. "Are you sure he didn't know any of the other people who were at church yesterday?"

She shook her head. "I'm sure." She leaned closer. "Do you realize what this means, Tess?" she asked tensely. "That note could have gotten Sherwood killed. At least, it'll prove somebody else could've had a motive. You have to turn it over to the police."

Tess nodded an agreement as the female officer walked over to the table. "Time's up."

Mavis sighed and rose to her feet. Suddenly she bent down to say into the speaker, "If my mother calls Iris House, don't tell her I've been arrested. I don't want her here. I can't deal with her on top of everything else."

Tess left the room, wondering how long Mavis thought she could keep her mother in the dark about her arrest. In the reception room, Curt and Madison were reading wanted posters.

"Wow, look at this guy, Curt," Madison said. "Heavy. I'd hate to run into him in a dark alley."

"Whoa. He's got crazy eyes."

"Is Officer Neill in?" Tess asked the officer at the desk.

"Not right now, ma'am. Can I help you?"

Tess fingered the note in her pocket. "No," she said. "I'll talk to him later." She walked over to Curt and Madison.

Madison pointed to a poster depicting a teenage girl. "Look at this, Tess. She's just sixteen. She was arrested for armed robbery and escaped from the jail."

"She looks scared to death," Curt put in.

Yes, she did, Tess saw. And no doubt she had been when that picture was taken, as frightened as Mavis Draper was now.

"Let's go, troops," Tess said.

"How is Mrs. Draper?" Madison asked as they left the station.

"Pretty depressed."

"Wouldn't you be?" Madison asked.

Tess agreed that she surely would. She was happy not to be in Mavis's shoes as she drove to the Christmas tree lot on Main Street where they chose an eight-foot Scotch pine. "I have no way to get it home," she told the lot owner. "Do you deliver?"

"I can do that," he said, "when my wife gets here to look after the lot. Six o'clock be okay?"

"Perfect," said Tess. It would give her time to rearrange a couple of pieces of furniture in the guest parlor to make room for the tree. More importantly, she'd have time for a talk with Bill Chandler.

## Chapter 13

After Curt helped Tess rearrange the parlor furniture, she found the box of tree decorations at the back of her closet. Leaving Curt and Madison to untangle several strings of lights and check them for burned-out bulbs, Tess drove to Bill Chandler's insurance office.

"He's meeting with a client," the receptionist told her.

"Is it okay if I wait?" Tess asked.

"Oh, he's not here. They're meeting at the client's place of business."

The weight of the note in Tess's pocket seemed to grow heavier with each passing minute. She should turn it over to Andy Neill before Mavis told her lawyer about it. She glanced out the office window at King Street, where passing traffic sprayed slush toward the curbs, and tried to decide what to do. "When do you expect him back?"

"I can't say. He said he might go straight home from the meeting. If you want to see him about an insurance policy, I can probably help you."

Tess shook her head. "No, thanks. I'll talk to him later."

After leaving the office, Tess sat in her car, turning the problem over in her mind. She could take Seventh Street three blocks east to the police station, or she could make one last stab at finding Bill at home. She started the motor and took Hill Street north, leaving the business district behind.

The Chandlers lived on the edge of town in an attractive residential area which was still expanding northward as new homes were built. The Chandler house, a two-story red brick with white shutters and a columned front porch, was a scaled-down version of a southern plantation house.

Claire answered the door. "Why, hello, Tess."

"Sorry to drop in unannounced."

Claire continued to stand in the doorway, one hand on the facing. "If you're here to talk about the Christmas pageant," she said dully, "I haven't even had a chance to think about it yet." The muscles in her face were slack and there were dark circles beneath her eyes. Concern over the pageant? Tess wondered.

"Don't be troubled about the Christmas pageant, Claire," Tess said. "We'll put something together later in the week. Actually, I didn't come about that. I came to see Bill. Is he in?"

Claire, her brows drawn in a tight frown, looked uneasy. "Yes, but he's not feeling well."

"I'm sorry," Tess said, "but it's imperative that I talk to him now."

"What about?" Claire's voice was tense. It was more than the Christmas pageant, Tess decided. What was wrong with Claire, for heaven's sake?

The temperature had risen into the forties, but it was still too cold to be kept standing on the porch indefinitely. "Could I come in, please, Claire?"

With clear reluctance, Claire stepped aside, let Tess in, and led the way from the foyer to a living room furnished with country French antiques. The house was quiet.

Claire turned to face Tess. "Now, what is this all about?"

"It's a matter of some—er, delicacy, Claire. Please tell Bill I'd like to see him."

Claire stared at her. "I don't understand what's going

on around here.'' Her voice rose querulously. Then she turned abruptly and stomped out, leaving Tess standing in the living room, wondering what had brought on Claire's last remark.

A few minutes later, Claire returned with her husband. "Hello, Tess,'' Bill said wearily. My God, he looked worse than Claire, who had folded her arms across her chest and stood like a post, waiting.

"I'm sorry to disturb you at home, Bill, but I did go to your office first,'' Tess said.

"It's all right. What can I do for you?''

She glanced at Claire, who glared back, spots of color burning in her cheeks. The atmosphere in the room was charged with tension. "May we speak in private?''

He frowned. "If this is an insurance matter—''

"It isn't,'' Tess said.

Claire spoke suddenly. "I can't imagine what you could have to say to Bill that I can't hear.''

Tess held Bill's gaze. "That's not my decision to make. Maybe Bill should hear me out before he decides.''

As though he'd read the urgency in Tess's face, Bill's eyes had the look of a man who'd received a jolt from an unexpected direction. Claire, who was watching him closely, clearly saw his apprehension, too. "Let's go into the study,'' he said.

Tess followed him into a large room with walls of dark oak library paneling and a corner fireplace where blue flames licked gas logs. An oak desk sat next to a wide window overlooking the backyard. A navy and wine plaid sofa sat against the opposite wall facing a square oak coffee table which held a stack of magazines.

Bill closed the door. "I've got a lot on my mind, Tess, so could we cut to the chase?''

She drew the note from her coat pocket. "I found this at church Monday evening.''

He stared at the note as if it were a snake that would surely bite him if he touched it. He swallowed hard and his Adam's apple bobbed. "What's that?''

"The message you tossed in the trash."

Before Tess could move back, the door flew open and Claire barged in and snatched the note from Tess's hand. "By God, I want to know what's going on around here!" Bill grabbed for the note, but she twisted away from him, turned her back and read, "You have twenty-four hours to do the right thing or I go to the police."

Bill reached around her and took the note. "This is none of your business, Claire!"

Claire swept a hand through her already disheveled hair. "What does it mean?" Her voice held an edge of hysteria.

"I have no idea," Bill said and handed the note back to Tess. "You've made a mistake, Tess. This wasn't meant for me."

"I saw you take it from your overcoat pocket," Tess said quietly.

"Oh, I don't deny it was in my pocket," Bill said in a rush, his words infused with a strained attempt at drollery, "but I doubt the kids knew whose pocket they put it in."

"What kids?" Tess asked.

"The teenagers who were at the church yesterday. They got bored and decided to play a practical joke. Isn't it obvious?"

"It doesn't sound like a joke," Claire murmured weakly.

"It's no joke," Tess agreed. "This note was written by Sherwood Draper. His wife identified the handwriting."

Nobody said anything for several moments. Bill's shoulders sagged and he turned away. Every muscle in Claire's body tensed. For an instant, she stood as if turned to stone, but her eyes, huge and stunned, flew to her husband. Then, abruptly, she stepped to his side and clutched his arm frantically. "Bill?"

"It's a mistake, Claire." Pulling free of her grasp, Bill glanced toward Tess and continued defiantly. "I didn't even know the man. And how could he have known which coat was mine? There were several overcoats hanging in the church foyer, and one overcoat looks much like another. He picked the wrong one.''

"Of course, that must be what happened," Claire said, looking at Tess with a flicker of relief in her eyes. "Denny Brookside has a gray overcoat like Bill's. The note must have been meant for him."

For the first time, Tess's certainty wavered. Claire was right. Denny Brookside did have a gray overcoat and Denny *had* known Sherwood Draper.

"I have to turn this over to the police, Bill," Tess said.

He jammed both hands into his trousers' pockets and drew in a gulp of air. "Why haven't you done it already?"

"I wanted you to know about it first."

He nodded stiffly. "That was thoughtful of you, but it has nothing to do with me."

"Perhaps I drew the wrong conclusion," Tess said. "If so, I'm sorry. I'll see myself out, Claire."

Tess walked quietly to the front door and paused to listen. No discernible sound came from the study. She let herself out.

Releasing a sigh of satisfaction, Tess dropped to the chintz sofa in the guest parlor to admire the Scotch pine. Topped by a white and gold angel, it was covered with multicolored sequined balls and a variety of wood ornaments which she had collected over the past several years. Gold, red, and green lights woven through the spreading branches flashed on and off merrily.

"It's beautiful," Tess sighed. "I love Christmas."

Luke sat down beside her and slipped an arm around her shoulders. He'd arrived after Tess had placed various Christmas decorations around the house and just as Tess, Curt, and Madison were putting the finishing touches on the tree, but in time to join them in Tess's apartment for hot buttered popcorn and spiced cider. By then it was close to eleven, and when they finished the snack, Tess had suggested it was time for Curt and Madison to go to bed.

Madison had looked at Curt and giggled. "*C'est adroit*! They want to be alone."

"That's cool. Whyn't you say so, Tess?" Curt asked. "I'm outta here." He left the apartment and bounded up the stairs to his room.

"Me, too," Madison said and headed down the hall to Tess's spare room, calling, "*Bonne nuit*. Have fun, kids!" over her shoulder.

"I think she said we're cute," Luke observed.

"That's what she said."

"Everybody's a comedian."

Whereupon, Tess had grabbed Luke's hand and led him back to the guest parlor for one more look at the tree. She had tried all evening not to think about the murder investigation, but she had failed miserably. She kept seeing Mavis, so helpless looking in those awful green coveralls. She had hoped the tree would distract her.

But Luke knew her moods too well. "Want to tell me what's been on your mind all evening?"

So she told him about the note, her visit to Mavis at the jail, her subsequent visit to the Chandlers, and about returning to the police station to deliver the note to Andy Neill.

"That should have given him second thoughts about arresting Mavis Draper," Luke mused.

"I think it did, but he wouldn't admit it. He insisted he had the murderer behind bars and he thought the D.A. would be willing to take the case to court." Neill had also told her that the only prints on the murder weapon were Tess's, where she'd gripped the shears to remove them from Draper's back in order to administer CPR. The murderer had obviously wiped them clean after stabbing Draper.

"Maybe he's right." He didn't sound convinced, but then he said, "Anyway, it's in the hands of the police now." He gave her a hard hug. "You did the right thing, taking the note to the police, sweetheart. Surely Neill will at least talk to Bill Chandler.''

"He said he would," Tess murmured, "but Bill insists the note wasn't meant for him. He and Denny Brookside both have gray overcoats and Bill says Draper must have put the note in his coat by mistake."

"Could be," Luke said. "Denny knew Draper. But I still can't think what Draper could have known about Denny that the police would be interested in. What do you think Draper meant by 'do the right thing'?"

Tess shrugged. "I haven't an inkling, and neither has Mavis. But obviously Draper wanted Denny—or whoever the note was meant for—to go to the police himself and—well, confess something."

"Wonder what it could be?"

"I can't even imagine," Tess admitted. "Denny runs a grocery store. I guess he could be falsifying tax returns or something."

"Denny Brookside? I don't believe it."

"Neither do I. And even if he was, how could Sherwood Draper have known about it?"

"Somebody told him?"

Tess shook her head. "Same problem," Tess mused. "How could that person have known? No, it's impossible."

He turned her toward him and kissed her. "We aren't going to figure it out tonight, love."

"Luke?" Her tone was thoughtful. "Bill and Claire Chandler are frightened of something. The tension in that house when I was there earlier today was as thick as molasses."

His hands clasping her shoulders, he tilted his head and peered down at her. "You must've shocked their socks off when you showed up with that note. They probably thought you were accusing Bill of being involved in something illegal."

Tess shook her head. "That upset them, all right, but

they were scared before I showed Bill the note. Something's going on in that house.''

"Maybe Neill can ferret it out.''

"Do you really think he'll try very hard?'' she asked dryly. "He's made an arrest. He's probably already let Butts know how efficiently he's handled the investigation. Case closed. I may have to look into it myself.''

He quirked an eyebrow. "Stay out of it, Tess.''

"I wish I could,'' she said sadly, "but if you'd seen Mavis Draper at the jail, you'd know why I can't.''

"Are you really sure she didn't kill her husband?''

"I'm not sure, no. But there are too many loose ends that should be looked into, and I'm afraid Neill won't do it. He doesn't want to find evidence on anybody besides Mavis.''

"Loose ends? Like that note, you mean.''

"Yes, and Sherwood Draper's last words. Nancy Howard. His dying words, Luke. They have to be important. We have to find out who Nancy Howard is.''

"How do you propose doing that, sweetheart?''

She chewed her lip thoughtfully. "I don't know yet, but I'll think of something.''

He chuckled. "I don't doubt it for a minute, love. Now, could we forget the murder investigation for a while?''

"I'll try.''

"I'll help you,'' he said, as he gently pushed against her shoulders until she was lying on the couch on her back. His handsome face hovered above hers. "Tess . . .''

He sounded so earnest, suddenly. "Yes?''

He hesitated. "Never mind. Now isn't the time.''

"The time for what?''

For an instant, he gazed at her, and then his serious expression was gone. "I see I finally have your attention.''

Tess gave him a wicked grin and wrapped her arms around his neck. "Yes, sweetheart.''

He nodded slowly. "Good. In case you haven't noticed, it's very quiet in the rest of the house.''

He smelled of Ivory soap and Polo aftershave, Luke scents. She took his face in both her hands. ''Now that you mention it,'' she murmured and pulled his head down until their mouths were a hair's breadth apart. ''I think our little chaperones are lost in dreamland.''

He kissed her slowly, thoroughly. ''I prefer to have my dreams while I'm awake,'' he said huskily. His blue eyes gazed deeply into her eyes, into her heart. ''You are incredibly beautiful,'' he whispered and kissed her again.

She was far from beautiful, but it was wonderful of him to say so.

## Chapter 14

Since there were no longer any paying guests in Iris House, Tess called Gertie Wednesday morning and told her she still didn't need to come to work. Tess could manage meals for Curt and Madison.

"I could use a couple of days to finish my Christmas shopping," Gertie said.

"I'll let you know if I get an unexpected booking."

"Good, and I'll come over next week, regardless, fix some things you can put in the freezer for your Christmas guests. You'll find it's a big job, keeping four additional people fed for two weeks."

"Especially when one of them's a thirteen-year-old boy," Tess observed.

"You bet. As for Christmas dinner, how many people are you expecting?"

"Let's see, besides my father, Zelda, and the kids, there's Aunt Dahlia and Uncle Maurice, Cinny, and Cody Yount. And Luke, of course. That's ten, including me." Tess had not actually added them up until now. She wasn't in the habit of preparing a meal for that many people, and she felt a little overwhelmed.

"The turkey will be easy, and I'll give you my recipe for the stuffing and a wonderful cranberry salad. I imagine the men will lounge around watching the football games all afternoon and evening. What time are you serving dinner?''

''Seven, I thought.''

''Then you'll need some finger foods for earlier in the day. We can fix those ahead and freeze them. And a couple of coffee cakes for breakfast Christmas morning.''

''You're a life saver, Gertie.''

Tess was in the big kitchen, where she'd prepared fruit cups and set out eggs and bacon for cooking when Curt and Madison put in an appearance. She had no sooner hung up the kitchen phone than Nedra Yates, her housekeeper, arrived through the back door. Tess heard her stomp mud off her shoes on the mat in the utility room, before she came into the kitchen.

''Figured you need me,'' Nedra announced. The housekeeper communicated with as few words as possible. Sometimes Nedra's brain got ahead of her mouth and she started speaking in the middle of a thought, but, after almost two years, Tess had learned to translate Nedra-talk pretty well.

''You better believe it,'' Tess told her.

Nedra slipped off her coat, revealing her usual work uniform of jeans and cotton shirt. Her straw-colored hair was pulled back into a pony tail and secured with several hairpins on each side. But no matter how many hairpins and rubber bands Nedra used to control her wild mop of hair, it would be flying every which way before the day was over.

Nedra helped herself to coffee from the pot Tess had made earlier and sat at the big oak kitchen table to drink it.

''Have you had breakfast?'' Tess asked.

''Yep.''

Tess got a cup of coffee and joined Nedra at the table.

''Professor got hisself killed.''

Tess nodded glumly.

Nedra blew on her coffee to cool it. ''Heard Andy Neill arrested the wife.''

"Yes, and I feel so sorry for that poor woman, Nedra. Can you imagine being in jail at Christmastime? Any time, for that matter."

Nedra shook her head. "Hired Cody Yount, huh?"

Not surprisingly, Nedra, like most everyone in Victoria Springs, was well informed on the case. Although thousands of tourists swelled the population during the season, it was still a small town and the year-round residents kept up with events and each other.

"Cody's good," Tess mused, then shook off an image of Mavis Draper behind bars. "At any rate, with what's happened to the Drapers, Madison and Curt are now my only guests, and they can pick up after themselves. Gertie's taking a few days off and you might as well, too, after today."

Nedra took a cautious sip from her cup. "Give the place a good cleanin'. Come back Saturday."

"That would be a big help. There'll be laundry to do by the weekend."

Madison and Curt came looking for Tess then, and Nedra went about her cleaning. Tess fixed two fried eggs and bacon for Curt. Madison opted for a piece of toast and bemoaned the fact that the local teenagers were back in school today and she was stuck with Curt for company. Curt told her to go write a letter to precious Danny boy. Madison told him to go suck a stump. Tess interrupted to say that she had a Monopoly game and a deck of cards, if they were interested. The brother-sister bantering continued after breakfast as Curt and Madison went to Tess's apartment for a game of Hearts.

A few minutes later, Tess was headed for the apartment herself when the front doorbell rang. It was Lily Brookside and she was in a snit.

Lily stormed past Tess and into the guest parlor, dramatically flinging off a red wool cape as she went. Beneath the cape she wore a black turtleneck sweater and black slacks. She tossed the cape on a chair. "I can't believe you, Tess Darcy!"

Tess closed the door and followed her. "Oh, dear. What have I done now?" Tess asked, trying for a light tone.

Lily was not amused. "You told the police Sherwood Draper threatened Denny!"

"I did no such thing! Who said I did?"

Lily paced restlessly across the parlor to a lace-covered window, glanced out, her brow furrowing. Then she turned to face Tess. "The police."

Tess sat down on the sofa. "Sit, Lily, and try to calm down. I gather you had a visit from Officer Neill."

Lily's attractive face was drained of its normal color, and the pink blusher Lily had applied to her high cheek-bones looked almost garish. She hesitated for a moment, then sat stiffly on the edge of a sculptured cane chair, her knees together, her hands gripping each other.

"Tell me exactly what Neill said," Tess encouraged.

"He told us Sherwood Draper had left a threatening note in an overcoat that looked like Denny's, but since the owner of the coat didn't know Draper, it must have been meant for Denny."

"Must have?"

"Well, he said, 'could have,' but it's practically the same thing." She gnawed nervously on a scarlet thumb-nail which showed evidence of having been nibbled on already today. "He said *you* found the note and turned it over to him." She looked at Tess anxiously. "The only other person with an overcoat the color of Denny's is Bill Chandler. Is that where you found it, Tess?"

"No," said Tess truthfully, "I found it in the trash can in the church foyer."

Lily looked puzzled. "But Neill said—" Her eyes narrowed. "You saw Bill throw it in the trash, didn't you?"

"You'll have to talk to Andy Neill about that, Lily. It's police business now."

She shot to her feet again and began to pace. "Oh, I see. You can't tell me what's going on, but you can tell the police that the note was meant for Denny when you

don't know that for a fact.'' She halted and glared at Tess.
''Do you?''

''I repeat, Lily, I did not tell anyone the note was meant
for Denny.''

''It was Bill and Claire then.'' She grabbed her cape.

''Wait a minute, Lily.'' Lily paused in the act of throwing on the cape. ''Please.''

She let the cape slide back onto a chair, but remained
standing.

Tess said, ''Bill and Denny were wearing those coats
Monday at the church. Andy Neill probably saw them
and, after learning that Sherwood Draper didn't know Bill
Chandler, remembered the matching coats and wondered
if the note was meant for Denny, who *had* met the professor before he arrived in Victoria Springs.'' No point in
revealing that it was Bill and Claire who'd mentioned the
similar coats originally. There was enough bad blood between Lily and Claire as it was.

Around one finger, Lily twisted a lock of black hair
that had escaped her French braid. ''Denny knew him, but
not well.'' She sighed and returned to the cane chair. ''I
know Denny was upset because Sherwood and I were
being—well, friendly with each other.'' She suddenly
looked miserable. ''Denny finally admitted to me that
he'd had a talk with Sherwood backstage and told him to
stay away from me. But mostly Denny blamed me, Tess,
not Sherwood. We had an awful row about it.'' She
blinked back tears.

''And there was no reason for Sherwood to threaten
Denny?''

She shook her head and her chin trembled. ''Neill
didn't show us the note, but he told us what it said. Something about doing the right thing or he'd go to the police.
Like whoever the note was intended for had committed a
crime. He couldn't possibly have written that to Denny.''
She drew in a shaky breath. ''My husband is not a criminal.''

''Even if he were''—Tess mused, half to herself, then

lifted a hand as Lily huffed a protest—"and I'm sure he isn't. I'm just saying *if*—how could Sherwood Draper have learned about it? As you say, he didn't know Denny very well. Whereas you know your husband better than anyone, and the note makes no sense to you."

As Tess spoke, Lily had sat with her head bowed. Now, she looked up, and tears spilled down her cheeks. "I thought I knew him inside out, Tess, but now—"

Tess crossed to the cane chair and put a comforting hand on Lily's shoulder. "Now what, Lily?"

She couldn't speak for several moments. Then, she choked out, "Denny has been acting so strange ever since—since Sherwood died. And he won't talk to me—really talk, I mean. I'm scared, Tess."

Tess gently squeezed Lily's shoulder. "The murder has thrown us all for a loop. Things will be back to normal before long." For almost everyone except Mavis Draper, at least.

Lily pulled a tissue from the pocket of her wool slacks and wiped her eyes. "Yes, you're right." She looked up at Tess. "The police haven't released Mavis Draper, have they?"

Tess shook her head. "Neill seems convinced she's the murderer."

"Well—" Lily wiped her eyes again and stuffed the tissue back in her pocket. "She did threaten to kill us both—Sherwood and me."

"Did you believe her at the time?"

Lily hesitated, then shook her head. "Not really. I've said those very words myself, when I'm mad at Denny or the kids. But that was before you found Sherwood with those shears in his back. Oh, it's all so awful." She shuddered. "I should go. I'm sorry for yelling at you, Tess. I'm just not myself today. I made a mountain out of a molehill." She got to her feet and reached for her cape again.

"Don't worry about it, Lily." Tess walked her to the door, but as she watched Lily get into her car and drive away, she thought Lily's reaction to the note was telling.

Lily was still terrified, and Tess could think of only one reason for Lily's fear. Denny had confronted Draper about his interest in Lily, and Lily wasn't completely convinced that her husband had stopped with a mere warning. Lily was horribly afraid that Denny had killed Sherwood Draper.

# Chapter 15

"I'm so glad I caught you at home, Tess," Mavis Draper said. Her voice was bleak with misery. "I had to beg to get to use the phone at all. They'll not let me get my hands on it again today."

"There are laws to protect prisoners' civil rights, Mavis. I think they're required to give you access to the phone on a regular basis. Talk to your lawyer about it."

"I will, but access to the phone is the least of my problems. I—I think I've been in shock since the arrest, and it's just starting to sink in what terrible trouble I'm in." Her voice shook. "You have to help me, Tess. There's nobody else."

"That's what your lawyer's for. Did you tell him about the note?"

"Oh, yes. I called him the next time I got to the phone, after you showed it to me. He was here again this morning and told me the police have the note now."

"I promised you I'd give it to them, Mavis. Withholding evidence in a police investigation is a crime."

"I understand that," Mavis wailed. Her voice had risen; she sounded beside herself. "Mr. Yount's going to file a petition with the court for my release, because he says the note is new evidence that wasn't

141

available when I was arrested, but he told me not to get my hopes up. The police say there's no proof the note is connected to Sherwood's murder, and I'm afraid the judge will agree with them.''

''Maybe not—''

''He already denied bail! Listen, Tess!'' she shrilled. ''The guard is motioning for me to get off the phone. Help me! *Please*!''

''There's nothing I can do, Mavis.''

''Find out who Sherwood wrote that note to. I don't think the police will go out of their way to do it. Whoever it was has to be the murderer—because *I didn't do it*!'' She was sobbing now. ''I can't talk any more—goodbye, Tess.''

''Mavis, wait—'' But she was gone.

Tess hung up, deeply troubled by the call, and went back to the apartment kitchen, where Madison and Curt were finishing up their umpteenth game of Hearts. Madison straightened the deck and slapped it down on the table and announced that she was bored. *''J'ai ennui!''* she complained.

''There are plenty of good books upstairs in the library,'' Tess said. ''Surely you could find something you'd enjoy reading.''

Madison made a face, looking as though she'd tasted something unsavory.

''Not even!'' Curt guffawed.

Madison gave her brother a fake smile. ''Let's walk to town, Curtie.''

''She *is* bored,'' Curt said. ''At home, she wants to be driven everywhere.''

''Sorry, but I can't take you now, Madison,'' Tess said. ''I have things to do here.''

''Come on, Curt,'' Madison begged. ''We'll dress warmly, and it's only a few blocks. We could drop in on Cinny at the bookshop.''

''What a good idea. Let me call her,'' Tess suggested. ''I'll see if she can take you to lunch.''

Madison beamed at her. *''Merci.''*

* * *

Lunch for Tess was warmed-over chicken and noodle casserole and a Coke. She really had nothing urgent to do, but she'd stayed behind when Madison and Curt left to meet Cinny at the Queen Street Bookshop because she was in no mood for making conversation over lunch. She couldn't get Mavis Draper's pathetic plea for help out of her mind.

She took a memo pad and pen from the desk in her office and, as she ate lunch, she jotted down questions to herself.

*Did Sherwood Draper put the note in the wrong coat?*

*If I wanted to leave a threatening note in somebody's pocket, wouldn't I make sure it was the right coat?*

*Yes!!!*

*If the note was for Bill Chandler, there's a past connection between them. Maybe that's why the Chandlers are so stressed out.*

*What's the Chandler-Draper connection?*

Tess read what she'd written, thought for a minute, then added, *If the note was for Bill and not Denny Brookside, why is Lily so afraid?*

She already surmised the answer to the last question. Denny was acting strange, according to Lily, and she feared the worst—that Denny was the murderer. Mulling it over, Tess could come up with no other answers. She went to the phone and called the Forrest house.

"How well do you know Claire and Bill Chandler, Aunt Dahlia?" Tess asked.

"I know Claire better than Bill. We've served on church committees together. Is this about that mysterious note Professor Draper left in Bill's coat pocket?"

Tess was not the least bit surprised by the question. Like most of the town's permanent citizens, Dahlia always knew everything that was going on around town or had gone on in the past. In Dahlia's case, Tess didn't know how she did it, for she never seemed to pry. Sometimes she thought Dahlia had invisible sensors that the rest of humankind lacked.

"Yes," Tess admitted.

"I heard the note was a threat of some kind."

"So I understand," Tess replied judiciously, "and I can't stop thinking about it."

"Well, it makes absolutely no sense to me. Claire says they never met Draper before this week. Has it occurred to you that the professor could have been mentally ill? He certainly seemed to me to have a god complex."

"An oversized ego doesn't make you insane," Tess said. "Mavis never mentioned anything about her husband having mental problems. And she doesn't know what the note means—she asked me to find out."

"Tess, dear, think about it. It's to her advantage to throw suspicion on someone else. She is under arrest, you'll recall. It would be much better for her case if it could be proved that Bill Chandler had some deep dark secret in his past that Draper somehow unearthed. On the other hand, if Sherwood Draper was a psycho, then Bill's supposed criminal past could be nothing but a madman's delusion."

"I just want to settle it in my own mind, one way or the other," Tess said. "Do you know how long the Chandlers have lived in Victoria Springs?"

"Let me think a minute. They moved here when Cinny was eight or nine years old. I remember because Claire assisted in Cinny's Sunday School class shortly after she arrived."

Tess did a quick mental calculation. "So that would be sixteen or seventeen years ago."

"Yes."

"Do you know where they lived before?"

"Denver, as I recall. Bill was a loan officer in a bank there before he got into insurance. I remember he and Maurice having several conversations about the banking business."

Something was niggling at the back of Tess's mind. "Thanks, Aunt Dahlia."

"I'm afraid I haven't been any help, but then I'm convinced Bill Chandler never heard of Sherwood Draper before last Monday."

"You're probably right, Aunt Dahlia. By the way, Cinny took Madison and Curt to lunch."

"Oh, good. It'll give the cousins a chance to get better acquainted."

Tess hung up her office phone and sat down on the padded window seat where Primrose was drowsing in the pale sunlight. The cat opened one eye to look at Tess, then stretched and pushed her head under Tess's hand for stroking.

"What is it about Denver that's bugging me, Primrose?" Tess murmured.

Primrose settled beneath Tess's hand and began to purr.

The Chandlers had once lived in Denver. The town where the Drapers lived was less than a hundred miles from Denver, but Tess didn't know how long they'd been there. Even if they'd been there sixteen or seventeen years ago when the Chandlers were in Denver, it meant nothing. But there was something—something she'd heard recently. Tess tried to dredge up the elusive memory.

She thought back to Sunday, when the Drapers had arrived at Iris House. They'd talked only briefly when she showed them to their suite, but nothing of any relevance to anybody in Victoria Springs was said. The conversation the next morning at breakfast was similarly useless for Tess's current concern. The next time she saw the Drapers was at church. She and Luke had walked into the foyer as Pastor Matt was introducing Sherwood Draper. He'd gone over Draper's background as an actor and, then, as director of a community theater. . . .

That was it! The community theater had been in Denver.

So. It was possible that the Drapers and the Chandlers had lived in Denver at the same time. Tess thought about that. She'd finally made a tenuous connection, but she was no closer to knowing what was behind the note than before.

Did Bill Chandler commit a crime when he was in Denver? If he was arrested, it would have been in the papers. If it had made a big splash, Sherwood Draper might have remembered it. But there was a quicker way to find out if Bill Chandler had a police record. Now, if Andy Neill would only cooperate.

Tess left Primrose asleep on the window seat, went back to her desk, dialed the police station, identified herself, and asked for Andy Neill.

She was on hold for a couple of minutes before Neill said, "Hello."

"It's Tess Darcy, Andy."

"What's happening?" He sounded mighty chipper today.

"I had a phone call from Mavis Draper this morning. She says her attorney's going to file a petition with the court to have the charges against her dropped, based on that note I found."

"Yeah, Yount'll probably file today. Waste of time, if you ask me, but lawyers file a lot of petitions they know will go nowhere."

Tess let that pass without comment. "I was wondering if you would do me a favor."

"What?" Suddenly he sounded cautious.

"It turns out that the Drapers and Bill and Claire Chandler all lived in Denver at one time."

"Still looking for an explanation for that note, huh?"

"Aren't you?"

"Uh—well, sure."

Liar, Tess thought. "Could you run Sherwood Draper and Bill Chandler through your computer? See if either of them has a record?"

"I'm way ahead of you, Tess."

Tess was surprised. "You mean you've already checked them out?"

"Yes, ma'am," Neill said smugly.

Evidently she'd misjudged him. "And?"

"Sherwood Draper was charged with sexual harrass-ment four years ago, by a department secretary at the junior college where Draper taught. The case was filed and later settled out of court."

"And Bill Chandler?"

"Zilch. The man never even got a traffic ticket."

"Oh."

"I don't know who Draper meant that note for, Tess, but it wasn't Bill Chandler. And before you ask, I checked out Denny Brookside, too. Now, he's got a sheet."

"Really? When? Where? What did he do?"

"Exceeded the speed limit. Twice, six years ago. Guess he learned his lesson, got rehabilitated. Nothing on him since." Neill laughed. He was having a fine time teasing her. "Nothing on Mavis Draper, either, till now. 'Course that's often the case with these crimes of passion. Anything else you need?"

"Not at the moment, Andy."

Damn Andy Neill. He had enjoyed telling her that she was wasting her time trying to help Mavis. Maybe she was, but Tess still wasn't satisfied. The Chandlers and the Drapers had both lived in Denver. The note had been in Bill's overcoat. And Bill and Claire were uptight about *something*.

So, what next?

Bluffing. It wasn't much, and it was a last resort. But what else was there?

Tess decided her best move was to talk to Claire and Bill separately. She'd show up at the Chandler house without phoning ahead. Claire was the weak link, and considering the state she was in the last time Tess saw her, surprise might rattle her into letting something slip.

She waited until one-thirty, giving Bill time to be back at the office in case he'd gone home for lunch. She'd given Madison and Curt a key to the front door and left a note on her apartment door, saying she'd be back soon.

Claire was not happy to see her. "We need to make plans for the Christmas pageant," Tess said. It got her in the door.

Claire offered her coffee. Tess accepted. When Claire returned to the living room with their cups and a small plate of butter cookies on a tray, she said, "I think we can use some of the stuff we used four years ago. There isn't time to put together a whole new pageant. Elizabeth Purcell has agreed to help me."

"That's great."

"We need to get Mike Tandy involved, too, of course. If he can get away from the store, I'd like to schedule a meeting Friday morning at the church."

"Sounds fine to me."

"We'll need costumes," Claire reminded.

"I can handle that."

Claire sank into a chair with a sigh. "It's best for all of us to get our minds back on the holidays, forget what's happened. It may sound unfeeling, yet life goes on."

"Unfortunately, we carry the past with us into the present," Tess mused.

Claire set her cup on the coffee table. "I suppose." She watched Tess thoughtfully. "Why are you looking like the cat who's been in the cream pitcher?"

Tess took a deep breath and said, "I know about Denver, Claire."

She frowned. "What about Denver?"

"You and the Drapers both lived there at one time."

Claire gave an explosive little laugh. "Really? Well, that's not exactly a hot news flash. What's your point, Tess?"

Tess had no idea what her point was, so she said nothing, waited for the silence to make Claire nervous enough to say more.

Claire finally spoke, but what she said was no help at all. "That was years ago, Tess. If you're suggesting we knew the Drapers back then, you're wrong. Denver is a big city."

So much for bluffs. And weak links.

\* \* \*

As she left the Chandler house, Tess wondered if it was worth trying to bluff Bill. Then, again, what did she have to lose? If she was going to do it, she'd better get to him before Claire did.

No doubt she was wasting her time, she thought as she parked in front of the building where Bill Chandler's office was located. Claire had had time to phone and forewarn him. Should she or shouldn't she?

Then she saw Bill walk briskly down the sidewalk and turn in at his office building. It was as good an omen as any.

Tess got out of her car. "Bill!"

He had reached the entrance. He turned around and walked toward her. "Hello, Tess."

"We need to talk," Tess said, joining him on the sidewalk.

His eyebrows lifted fractionally. "Decided you need more insurance? An umbrella policy, maybe?"

She shook her head. "I know about Denver, Bill."

She knew she'd hit a nerve the instant the words were uttered. Bill Chandler flinched and his hazel eyes blazed, then hardened. "Let's go into my office," he said grimly.

Wordlessly, Tess followed him into the building, through the reception area where he merely nodded at the woman at the desk, and into his office. He closed the door.

"Let's get one thing clear," he snapped. "I will sue you if you've told anyone about this."

"You can't sue someone for speaking the truth," Tess responded with more confidence than she felt. "And the police must be told."

His next words stunned Tess. "I've already explained the whole thing to Andy Neill." So, Neill was more devious than she'd realized. He hadn't shared everything he knew about the case. Far from it. Now, if only she knew what Bill had *told* Neill.

"—but Claire doesn't know, and I don't want her to." His voice was tense. "It was a long time ago, Tess. I made a terrible mistake, but I made it right, put it behind me."

"If you made it right, as you say, why did Sherwood Draper threaten you with the police?"

He studied her for a long moment, then drew his breath in sharply. He went to the window and adjusted the wood blind before he said, "When I found that note in my pocket, I thought it was a joke." He looked at her sharply. "If I'd thought it was meant for me, do you think I'd have discarded it?"

Good question, and Tess had already wondered about that. "So it was only later that you realized it was for you?"

He nodded. "It was a while before I remembered that Draper had once lived in Denver and thought he might have put the note in my pocket. *Might* have, Tess. But I told the truth when I said I'd never met him before he came to Victoria Springs and I couldn't figure out how he knew about Denver. There is no record anywhere. I resigned and worked out a payment schedule with the bank. They agreed not to press charges. It would've been bad for business. It took five years, but I made full restitution plus interest." He walked behind his desk and sat down heavily. He stared at his hands resting on the polished surface of the desk.

Tess let his words sink in and then she understood. He'd embezzled money from the bank where he'd worked. "I can see how an embezzlement charge might have made it difficult to find other employment."

He sat very still for a moment, then looked up at her. "We were living above our income. We'd bought an expensive house and a speed boat, and I was having trouble meeting the payments. I only meant to borrow the money and pay it back as I could." His face crumpled. "I know I'm not the first embezzler to tell myself that. If this gets out, Tess, my business could be ruined."

Yes, people would have second thoughts about an insurance advisor who'd stolen money from his employer.

"I would have talked to Draper, explained that there was no need to go to the police because I'd made restitution." He lifted both hands in a gesture of futility. "He was killed before I had the chance."

Talking to Draper would have been the sensible thing to do, and Bill Chandler was nothing if not sensible. Would Draper have let it drop there? What reason would he have had for taking it further? Sure, he could have hurt Bill's insurance business, but why would he want to harm a man he didn't know? After all those years, why threaten Bill with exposure?

More to the point, how could Sherwood Draper have known about the embezzlement in the first place if there was no record of it? Bill's fear that Claire would learn the secret he'd kept from her so many years had made him assume the note was for him, but it didn't quite hang together for Tess. She was no longer sure the note had been meant for Bill.

"Have you told anyone else what you know?" he asked.

Tess shook her head and his shoulders sagged with relief. No wonder Bill Chandler had been so worried lately. He was afraid his past would come back to haunt him after more than fifteen years. But there was an air of resignation, too, as if he'd already decided how he'd handle it if news of his past crime got out. That's the kind of man Bill Chandler was, the kind who in a crisis asked himself, What's the worst that could happen? and then he'd figure out how he'd cope if it did.

Moreover, Tess didn't sense any real guilt in him. Surely if a law-abiding man—at least one who'd been law-abiding for seventeen years—if such a man had taken a life in a moment of panic, he would be burdened by remorse.

"If it becomes public knowledge, it won't be because of me," Tess added. "Thank you for being honest with me, Bill."

## Chapter 16

Tess had been home a half-hour when Cinny brought Madison and Curt back to Iris House.

"I can only stay a few minutes," Cinny told Tess. "We're doing a brisk business at the bookshop today. When people can't think of anything else for Christmas gifts, they settle on books."

"Lucky for you," Tess said.

"Indeed."

"Are the Christmas baskets moving?" Tess asked. Cinny's baskets contained a mug, individual packets of tea and coffee, a small packet of Swiss chocolates, a bookmark, and two or three books with a Christmas theme.

"Flying out the door," Cinny said, looking pleased with herself. She'd never worked a day in her life before her parents bought the bookshop for her. Everybody who knew Cinny had thought being in business was nothing but a passing whim, but Cinny was turning into a good businesswoman, even if she still hadn't conquered her tendency to be tardy. Fortunately, she had an assistant who opened the bookshop on time.

"I've done more business the first week of December than I usually do in a full month," Cinny continued, shrugging off her jacket. She sat in the blue armchair in Tess's sitting room and tucked her long blond hair behind her ears.

"Good for you," Tess said. "December's a slow month in the b-and-b biz. Along with January and February." In spite of a tight budget, Tess actually enjoyed the lack of business during the off-season. It gave her a chance to catch her breath and gear up for the flood of tourists that would begin in March. "Would anybody like something to drink?"

Madison flopped down on the couch. "Don't mention food," she groaned. "I'm stuffed."

"Nothing for me, Tess," Cinny said.

"Maybe I'll have a Coke," Curt announced and bolted for the kitchen.

"Does that child ever get full?" Cinny inquired.

"No," said Madison.

"For lunch," Cinny went on, "he had the Sampler Tearoom's chicken pot pie with a double order of French fries and blackberry cobbler a la mode. The pot pie alone is enough for two normal people."

"Nobody ever said Curtie's normal," observed Madison.

"Gertie keeps reminding me he's a growing boy," Tess said.

Madison got to her feet. "With a serious tapeworm," she quipped. "Listen, thanks for lunch Cinny. I think I'll write some letters."

When she'd gone, Cinny remarked, "They're good kids."

"Uh-huh," Tess agreed.

Primrose padded into the room, went straight to Cinny, and wailed pitifully.

Cinny looked alarmed. "What's wrong with her?"

"You're in her chair," Tess said.

"Well, excuse me, your highness," Cinny said and patted her knee. "Come up and share it with me."

Primrose hopped into Cinny's lap and curled up. Stroking the soft gray fur, Cinny asked, "Is Mavis Draper still in jail?"

"Yeah. The judge denied bail. Apparently he thought she was a flight risk. She looks so pitiful behind bars."

"You've visited her?"

"Yes."

"What's this I hear about a threatening note that Professor Draper supposedly wrote to Bill Chandler?"

"There was a note," Tess said, "but I'm not sure it was meant for Bill Chandler. Evidently the Chandlers never set eyes on Sherwood Draper before Monday."

"I don't think anybody had, except for the Brooksides." Cinny's blue eyes narrowed. "Could the note have been meant for one of them?"

Tess shrugged. "In the note, Draper threatened to go to the police if whoever didn't do the right thing—whatever the right thing is. What has Lily or Denny ever done that the police would give two figs about?"

"Good question." Cinny pondered for a moment. "So who *did* Draper threaten?" She shook her head. "Actually, it was a kind of blackmail. Draper knew something damaging about somebody who was at the church Monday. And that means he knew them, or knew an awful lot about them."

"He knew them," Tess mused, "and clearly disliked them. Or at least felt they'd gotten away with something criminal. He meant to see that justice was done." Tess spoke slowly, as the idea took shape in her mind. Once said, though, she realized it was the only thing that made sense.

Cinny's eyes widened. "So they murdered him to keep him from going to the police."

"It makes sense, doesn't it?"

Cinny nodded.

"What bothers me is that Draper didn't seem like a crusader. Why would he get involved in the first place? Why did it matter so much to him?"

"Maybe he was already involved."

"What do you mean?"

"Maybe the injustice was done to *him*." Cinny pondered for a moment. "And if that's true, it wasn't Mavis Draper who killed him, was it?"

"I don't think so."

Cinny studied her carefully. "Don't be mysterious, Tess. Who *do* you think it was?"

"Haven't a clue," Tess admitted.

Cinny looked deflated. "Can't the police check out records on everybody who was at the church Monday? If one of them committed a crime and then—oh, I don't know, escaped from jail or something—wouldn't they have a record of it?"

"I'm sure they could check, given enough time," Tess said. Actually, it wasn't a bad idea. Neill had only looked for police records on the Drapers, Bill Chandler, and Denny Brookside. She wondered how hard it would be to check out everybody who was present when Sherwood Draper was murdered.

When Cinny left a few minutes later, Tess phoned Andy Neill and asked him that question.

"Waste of time, Tess," was Neill's response.

"Isn't it true that a lot of investigative work turns out to be a waste of time?"

"Yeah, sure, but we already got the murderer."

"What if you're wrong? Butts will never let you live it down."

"Hell, you would have to bring the chief into it." He sighed heavily. "Tell you what, Tess. I'll give that list of names to the department secretary. She can run them through the computer as she has the time."

"Thank you, Andy. It's always best to be thorough."

"Right," he muttered and hung up.

She looked in on Madison, who was still writing letters. Curt had gone up to his room. When Tess knocked on his door a few minutes later, the television was on—sounded like a talk show. "Just wanted to see if you have any plans for the rest of the afternoon," she said.

He sprawled on the bed. "Naw. I've been running the channels. Nothing worth watching." He picked up the remote control and turned off the set.

"I'm going up to the library. Want to come?"

"Sure."

From the end of the second-floor hall, they took the circular staircase up to the tower. Pale sunlight filtered through white undercurtains which draped the curving, floor-to-ceiling windows of the library. Tess hosted Victorian teas for her guests on Sunday afternoons during the season, but she hadn't been up to the tower in almost three weeks, since before Thanksgiving.

White wicker furniture, its fat cushions covered with chintz featuring purple daisies, pink irises, and bright green foliage vining across a white background, was arranged on the green rug in a conversational grouping in the center of the library. Opposite the windows were four sections of floor-to-ceiling bookshelves.

"This is way cool," Curt exclaimed.

"It is, isn't it? The library's one of my favorite rooms in the house, but I haven't used it much lately."

Curt began scanning titles.

"The books are arranged by type," Tess told him. "Nonfiction in the left-hand section, then general fiction, then mystery and suspense. Science fiction, romance, and westerns are in the right-hand section."

Curt moved to the latter section while Tess found the old set of encyclopedias that had belonged to Aunt Iris. There was something she'd been meaning to look into ever since she'd had that conversation with Mavis Draper, the evening after the murder. A small loose thread to be tied up. It was the only track left to follow, though it would probably lead nowhere.

But she'd learned what she could about Sherwood Draper's note before she turned it over to the police, and had unearthed Bill Chandler's secret past, which was apparently a dead end. Andy Neill had promised to have the secretary run the other names through the police computer, but that could turn out to be another dead end, and even if something interesting was turned up, it could be days before she knew.

None of that seemed to have anything to do with Sherwood Draper's dying words, however, and they stayed at the back of Tess's mind, like an irritating thorn that couldn't be dislodged. *Nancy Howard*.

The only Nancy that Mavis Draper could think of was Sherwood's long-dead sister. Tess knew that his sister had been on Draper's mind the day of the murder, for he'd said Madison reminded him of Nancy. And he'd looked up at Madison in the doorway as he said the words. *Nancy*, a pause, and then *Howard* or something close to that. Had Draper been referring to his sister? And, if so, why had he added "Howard"? Tess suddenly had an off-the-wall idea. Perhaps Nancy Draper had been married secretly, a fact which Sherwood Draper had failed to mention to his wife.

Whether she had been married or not, Nancy Draper had been dead for more than twenty years, yet she'd been weighing on her brother's mind that day. Why? Tess thought the cause was more than the fact that Madison resembled her.

Okay, so what did she know about Nancy Draper? She had died in a car crash caused by a drunk driver, Mavis had said. It had happened at the University of Maine, where Nancy had been a student.

Tess pulled out the "M" volume of the encyclopedia, looked up "Maine, University of," and read the brief entry.

*A coeducational, state-supported school in Orono, ME. Also has four-year campuses in Farmington, Fort Kent, Machias, Portland-Gorham, and Presque Isle. The institution was founded in 1865, as the State College of Agriculture and Mechanic Arts, and was given its present name in 1897.*

She read it twice, then closed the volume thoughtfully. There must have been something about the wreck in the newspaper at the time it happened. She had no idea how to find such an article, but reference librarians existed to answer questions like that. The article would be easier for a librarian to track down if she knew which campus of the university Nancy Draper had attended. Perhaps Mavis could tell her.

She reshelved the encyclopedia volume. "Find anything interesting?" she asked Curt, who was leafing through a science fiction novel.

"Yeah, this one looks good. Can I take it to my room?"

"That's what they're here for," Tess said. She moved to the third section of shelves and found the first Henry-O mystery, *Dead Man's Island*, written by a favorite author, Carolyn Hart. "I'll take this to Madison."

"Why bother?" Curt asked.

"If I can get her to read the first few pages, I can almost guarantee she'll be hooked."

"If you get Madison to read a whole book, Mom will be grateful forever. She's always trying to coax Mad to read."

"Reading is such an enjoyable pastime. I hate for Madison to miss out on it."

"That's what Mom says. She used to read to us all the time, and we went to the library every week. It's supposed to make kids readers for life, according to Mom." He shrugged. "It didn't work with Madison."

"Sometimes people become readers later in life."

He grinned. "You're an optimist, aren't you?"

# Chapter 17

"Can you and the kids come over for dinner?" Luke asked without preamble when Tess answered the phone. It was after six, and she'd just been wondering what she could throw together for the evening meal.

"Don't tell me you're going to cook," Tess said with a laugh. "Not that you couldn't, if you set your mind to it." She'd learned that Luke could do anything he was determined to do. "It's just that I didn't think you liked to cook."

"Don't worry, hon, I'm not cooking. I'm getting takeout from the deli in Denny Brookside's supermarket. Nothing fancy. Chicken, baked beans, slaw."

"Sounds heavenly," Tess said. "I haven't had a chance to think much about dinner. I've been on the phone, first cajoling the jailer into letting me talk to Mavis Draper, and then with a couple of research librarians."

"How's Mavis holding up?"

"Not very well. She's sure the police aren't pursuing any leads that might exonerate her."

"You said you'd been talking to librarians. What are you researching?"

She told him about the car crash that had killed Sherwood Draper's younger sister so many years ago, adding, "Mavis told me that the girl was a student at the University of Maine in Orono, and I'm trying to find newspaper articles written at the time about her death. If I were in Maine, it would be much easier."

"Where in Maine?"

"The state historical society. One of the librarians said most of them keep old state newspapers on file."

"You don't need to be in Maine to check that out."

"I know. I'll look for a phone listing for the historical society tomorrow. I'm sure they'll search for the articles and, if they find any, mail me copies for a fee."

"We can make a search tonight, after dinner."

"The historical society won't be open that late."

"Forget all that. Wake up, dear Tess. We live in the electronic age."

"Meaning?"

"Computers. The World Wide Web. Surely you've heard of it."

"You mean you can look up old newspaper files on your computer?"

"Maybe not the complete file of every single newspaper in existence, but I wouldn't bet against it, either. The Internet is a vast universe of information, sweetheart. You really should get a computer and get online."

"One of these days," she said, "when I have the time."

"You've been saying that ever since I met you."

"And I mean it, too." The fact was if she had an extra three thousand dollars lying around, she could find a dozen other things she needed more urgently than a computer and printer. For example, new carpeting in the Carnaby Room, where a guest had come down with the flu and upchucked on the beautiful rose-colored carpet. Fortunately, a strategically placed chair hid the stain.

"See you later, then," Luke said.

"Wow, this is *so* incredible," Curt exclaimed. After dinner, Luke had put him and Madison at one of the three computers in his office, converted from what was once a den at the back of the house he'd inherited from his parents. Luke had logged onto the Internet and turned the computer over to Curt. Curt and Madison used computers in school, of course, but they didn't have access to the Internet.

"Hey, Tess," Curt said, "did you know there's something called yellow pages in here? You can type in any subject and it'll look up stuff for you."

"Amazing," Tess said.

"Type in something," Madison said impatiently. "How about a movie star—like Brad Pitt."

"You can look Brad up later. I'm trying 'books.' "

"My gosh," Madison yelped. "Look at that list. It's huge."

"Let's try Bookpage," Curt said, moving the mouse to click on the word.

Tess leaned over Luke's shoulder, as he searched for the Maine Historical Society on another computer. His fingers flew over the keys, bringing up site after site. It really was astounding. Maybe she *could* find the money for a computer, after all, Tess thought, and the time to learn to use it.

Tess knew that Luke and Sidney used the Internet frequently in their work, reading business publications, tracking stocks, keeping up with the markets during the trading day. Glancing across the room at Curt and Madison, she asked, "The Internet uses a phone line, doesn't it?"

"That's right," Luke said.

"But you're on it all day and sometimes in the evening. Isn't it terribly expensive?"

"I'm signed on with an outfit that gives me unlimited Internet time for twenty bucks a month."

"Oh," Tess murmured.

"I think I'm on the right track now." Luke typed something, then sat back to wait for a website to appear on the screen.

"Hey, Tess," Madison said, "what's the name of the author who wrote that book you gave me?"

"Carolyn Hart."

"Yeah. We found her name on the net. There's some stuff here about her. She lives in Oklahoma, and she's published lots of books and won a bunch of awards."

"I told you she was good," Tess said.

"Hmm," Madison said. "Maybe I'll start on that book tonight."

Curt cut his eyes around at her disbelievingly, but refrained from uttering his thoughts.

"Type in Brad Pitt now," Madison urged. After a moment, she said, "Oh, look. He's got a fan club and everything."

"Yeah, yeah—" muttered Curt.

"Wait! Let me read this."

Curt flopped back in his chair to allow Madison to scroll down the screen, picking up tidbits about Brad Pitt.

"Got it!" Luke said suddenly. "Maine Historical Society. And here's newspaper files—and Orono . . . What year are you interested in?"

"Mavis thought it was 1976."

Luke typed that in along with 'Nancy Draper,' and they waited for the results of the search. After a few moments, several lines of type appeared on the screen.

"Bingo," Luke said.

Tess counted the references. There were eight of them. "That's a lot of articles about one car crash. Can we read them?"

"I think so." He clicked on the first reference and shortly the article came on the screen.

Tess bent close to read.

"It'll be easier to read if I print it out," Luke said, bringing down a menu from the top of the screen and clicking on "Print." "It'll take several minutes to get all of them." The laser printer started humming and slowly, a sheet of paper began to emerge.

Tess and Luke had taken the articles into Luke's kitchen, leaving Curt and Madison surfing the net in the office. Luke made cappucino while Tess arranged the articles in order by date. The first one had a small, grainy picture of Nancy, a dark-haired young woman. Perhaps she resembled Madison, but the photo wasn't clear enough to tell. Tess read the article aloud.

### UNIVERSITY STUDENT DIES IN CRASH

Nancy Draper, 18, a freshman at the University of Maine, was killed last night when the car in which she was a passenger failed to make the curve in Highway 2 a mile north of Orono and flipped over twice. The driver, Howard Heisman . . .

Tess darted a look at Luke, who carried their cappucinos to the table. "The driver was named Howard! That's what the professor was trying to say when he died."

"Could be," Luke agreed. "But why?"

Tess shook her head. It made no sense to her, either. She continued reading.

. . . Howard Heisman, 20, a junior at the university, suffered a broken leg. He was treated at a local hospital and released.

Tess frowned and picked up the second article.

### DRIVER OF DEATH CAR CHARGED

Howard Heisman, 20, was in court today for a pretrial hearing on a charge of negligent homicide in the death of Nancy Draper, 18, a passenger in Heisman's car when it crashed on Highway 2 north of Orono about 1 a.m. November 3. In court yesterday, Prosecutor Adam Edelman presented the results of blood tests taken the night of the crash which showed Heisman's blood alcohol level to be in the "highly intoxicated" range. According to expert testimony a subject testing .15 or more alcohol in the blood is judged to be under the influence and unfit to operate a motor vehicle. According to statements from two of Heisman's fraternity brothers, eight students left the fraternity house in three cars after a beer party. Heisman had challenged two other men to a race around Dead Man's Curve, the name given by locals to the curve in Highway 2 a mile north of Orono where several wrecks have occurred. According to both statements, Nancy Draper was the only one of the group who hadn't been drinking. Heisman refused to listen to Draper's pleas to stay at the frat house. The three drivers stopped outside town to discuss the race, deciding to take the curve one at a time while somebody on the ground timed them with a stop watch. Heisman volunteered to go first. At that point, Draper got out of Heisman's car. "Howard got mad and called her a coward and dragged her back into the car. Nancy was crying and begging him not to race," according to the statement of Mark Anberg, 21. Heisman was bound over for trial on January 18.

The small photo accompanying the article showed an attractive young man with a lean face and dark hair. "Sounds like Heisman forced Nancy into his car against her will," Tess said, taking a sip of her cappucino. "That must have been hard for Nancy's parents to hear. Mavis said they never got over her death. They both died not long afterward."

Luke reached for the next article in the stack and

scanned it. "Here's a report on the trial. Heisman was convicted of negligent homicide. According to this, the penalty is from five to twenty-five years in prison and whatever fine the judge decides is appropriate. It says the judge would impose sentence the following week, Heisman to remain free on bail until then."

Tess glanced at the next article. The headline made her grab it and scan it quickly. "Listen to this, Luke."

CONVICTED FELON DISAPPEARS

Howard Heisman, convicted last week of negligent homicide in the death of Nancy Draper, University of Maine freshman, failed to appear in court for his sentencing. Officers dispatched to his fraternity house were told Heisman had packed up and left the previous day. According to those questioned, Heisman gave no indication of where he was going. Heisman's mother told police she hadn't seen or talked to her son for three days. Heisman's father, reportedly living in New York, could not be reached for comment. Heisman was sentenced to twenty years in the state penitentiary in absentia and a fugitive warrant was issued for his arrest. Anyone with any information on Heisman's whereabouts is asked to contact the police at 555-6083. Heisman is 6 feet tall, weighs 170 pounds, and has a two-inch scar from a childhood accident running diagonally across his chin. Since the wreck which totaled Heisman's car, he has been driving a blue Ford sedan registered to his mother, Agnes L. Heisman Bangor.

The accompanying photo was the same one published previously.

Luke perused the next article. "This was written a year

later. Heisman still hadn't been apprehended. His mother's car was found in a shopping center parking lot in Philadelphia three weeks after his disappearance and returned to her. Listen to this. The mother says she got a call in the middle of the night from her son, telling her where to find her car. He wouldn't say where he was and she hasn't heard from him since."

"Then, it's possible Howard Heisman is still at large," Tess mused.

Luke laid the article he'd read aside. "The next one's six months after that. Heisman still missing." He leafed through the remaining articles, all of which were recaps of the case and Heisman's disappearance. The last one was dated almost three years after the event. At that point, Heisman was still a fugitive. After scanning the article, he handed it to Tess.

"This is unbelievable," Tess said. "How can someone just disappear?"

"Probably happens more often than you realize," Luke said.

"No wonder Nancy's parents grieved themselves to death. Not only did they lose their only daughter because of this Heisman's recklessness, he was never made to pay for what he'd done."

"As far as we know," Luke observed.

Tess nodded, thinking. "But, surely, if Heisman was ever caught, there would have been an article about that, too."

Tess thought she knew how to find out for sure.

# Chapter 18

Tess waited until ten the next morning to place a call to the Orono newspaper in which the articles had appeared. She used the phone in her office, since Curt and Madison had a hot game of Monopoly going in the kitchen. She asked to speak to a crime reporter and was switched to another line. A gruff-sounding man answered with a bark.

"Bloody hell!"

For an instant, Tess was speechless.

"Anybody there?"

"Yes—sorry. Who is this, please?"

"Brundy Helm, like I said."

Tess stifled a laugh. "Sorry, I—er, didn't understand."

"So, what'd you want?"

"I'm interested in a series of stories your paper published from 1976 to 1979."

"You want the morgue."

"Wait!" Tess cried, before he could cut her off. "I already have the articles. I'm looking for additional information about the Howard Heisman case."

"Doesn't ring a bell."

"He was a student at the University of Maine. He got drunk and wrecked his car. The girl who was with him was killed. Heisman was convicted and given a twenty-year sentence, but he disappeared. The last article your paper ran on it was in '79 and Heisman was still missing.''

"Yeah, now it's coming back. I wasn't here then, but I heard a couple of the old-timers talking about it. What's your interest in the case?"

Tess explained briefly that Nancy Draper's brother had been murdered while visiting her town. Then she repeated the professor's dying words. "He may not have been referring to Howard Heisman at all, but his wife can't think of anybody else it could be. She asked me to find out if Heisman was ever caught." Tess decided to leave out the fact that Mavis Draper was under arrest for her husband's murder.

"I'm gonna put you on hold for a minute," he said and did so before Tess could respond. A full two minutes later, he came back. "I talked to one of the guys who was with the paper then. Heisman was never apprehended, as far as he knows. Give me your phone number and I'll get back to you if I learn different."

Tess gave him the number. One question had been answered, she thought, not that she could see how it would aid Mavis Draper. "Thank you for your help, Mr. Helm."

"Look, I don't know what you're *not* telling me, but do me a favor."

"If I can."

"If it turns out that Draper's murder is connected to his sister's death, give me a call and I'll do a story on it."

"I will, and thank you again, Mr. Helm."

Tess picked up the newspaper articles and carried them to the window seat. She read them all again and stared at the picture of Howard Heisman for long moments, as if hoping he might open his mouth and speak. Tell her why he ran away, where he ran to, where he was now.

She tried to imagine being twenty years old and facing a prison sentence. He must've panicked as the sentencing date approached, bolted, and kept running.

How did a person disappear without a trace?

First, he moved far from where he was known, perhaps even left the country. Took a new name. Changed his appearance. If he had dark hair, like Howard Heisman, he probably became a blond. Once enough time had passed and he felt safe, he could have let his hair go back to its natural color. After more than twenty years, he would look much different, anyway. He might have gained weight and gone gray—a certainty if anxiety contributed to gray hair. He must have lived in a state of anxiety for years.

All of this was pure speculation, but it seemed reasonable to Tess as she gazed out the bay window. Sunday night's snow was gone, except for a narrow strip at the edge of the yard where drifts had piled high against the wrought iron fence.

A telephone call from Lily Brookside interrupted her musing.

"I'm looking for chaperones for the sock hop in the Church basement tomorrow night," she said. "Could you and Luke possibly oblige?"

"I can," Tess said. "I can't speak for Luke, but I'll ask him."

"Oh, thank you, Tess. The Tandys have agreed to chaperone, but we need another couple."

"I thought you and Denny would be there." The Brooksides always chaperoned the church's teen parties and Tess had been meaning to ask them to keep an eye on Madison and Curt for her.

"Denny's decided to be contrary," Lily complained. "He wants me to resign from all my church and country club activities. I'm sure he'll get over it in time, but the mood he's in right now, I don't want to defy him. Besides, I don't want to go to the kids' party alone and have to explain why he's not with me."

It sounded as if Denny still hadn't forgiven Lily for her indiscretion. "I'm sorry, Lily."

"Not your fault." She paused, then blurted, "I don't

know what to do about Denny, Tess. He comes home from the store and buries his head in a book. Expects me to sit here all day and then won't talk to me when he gets home. The kids keep asking me what's wrong with him. I'm running out of excuses.''

"He'll come around eventually, Lily. Give him time."

As Tess hung up, Curt yelled from the kitchen, "Hey, Tess, what's for lunch?"

# *Chapter 19*

At the sock hop Friday night Luke maneuvered to an open spot on the dance floor and threw Tess two arms' lengths away from him, then brought her back with a flourish.

She laughed. "Show off," she shouted. She had to shout to be heard above the music blaring from the CD player.

Moments later, quiet descended on the fellowship hall as somebody switched CDs. "I need a cold drink," Tess panted.

"Me, too." Luke led the way to one end of the hall where several tables had been set up. They chose two soft drinks from the big ice chest provided by the Tandys for the occasion and joined Blanche and Mike at a table for four.

The music started again. The four chaperones leaned toward the center of the table in order to hear each other.

"I'm convinced this whole generation of teenagers will be hearing impaired by the time they're twenty-one," Blanche shouted.

"Maybe we should all invest in hearing aid companies," Luke observed.

"There's a thought," Mike said.

Tess was watching the teenagers dance. Madison was apparently a hit, having been partnered with most of the boys in attendance. At the moment, she was side by side with Curt, teaching him some steps. Eddie Zoller swung by their table with a petite, red-haired girl whom Tess had seen at church the last few Sundays. "Eddie seems to be having a good time."

"He's wired," Mike said indulgently. "Been looking forward to tonight for weeks."

"You two," Luke said to the Tandys, "are the best thing that ever happened to that kid. I hope he appreciates it."

Blanche laughed. "Are you kidding? He's thanked us so many times it's embarrassing. Swears he'd have been in jail by now if we hadn't come to his rescue." She looked faintly troubled for an instant. "Mike, I haven't had a chance to tell you this yet, but today, when I asked Eddie if he'd made an appointment with the school counselor to talk about college scholarships, he said he's been thinking about staying on at the hardware store for a year or two after high school, said he wants to save some money."

"I told him we could help with his expenses," Mike said, "but I could use him full-time at the store if that's what he wants to do."

"Some kids need a year or two after high school to grow up," Luke put in.

"If Eddie doesn't go straight to college from high school," Blanche said, "I wonder if he'll ever go." She glanced at Mike. "And I don't think saving money is the main reason he wants to delay. The counselor told me she was sure he would qualify for a full scholarship. But we're the first security he's ever known, and I think he's afraid to give that up."

Mike's thick eyebrows lifted fractionally. "You're saying 'we' but you're looking at me."

"You're the father he never had," Blanche said. "Eddie idolizes you. We can't let him give up college to stay at the store with you. He'll be there when you're old enough to retire if we don't boot him out."

Mike shrugged. "I'll talk to him. Matter of fact, he *has* been hovering around me more than usual, and I know I've been a little short with him a couple of times. I'll make it up to him." He looked at Tess. "Hey, they've put on a slow one. My kind of music. Want to dance, Tess?"

Dancing with Mike Tandy was like being embraced by a friendly bear, but he was surprisingly light on his feet. His beard tickled her temple. She moved her head fractionally.

"Good of you and Luke to fill in for the Brooksides," Mike said.

"I must admit I was glad of the chance to keep an eye on Madison and Curt. They came with Boyd and Brenda, and I don't want Madison and Boyd slipping away from the party for a drive."

Mike grinned. "I noticed Boyd's real taken with your little sister. How old is she?"

"Fourteen," Tess said. They watched Madison and Boyd dance by, Madison's head tilted as she smiled coquettishly at her partner.

"Going on twenty," Mike added.

Tess grinned. "Believe me, I don't envy her mother for the next few years."

"Back to the Brooksides," Mike said after a moment. "Did Lily say why they couldn't chaperone?"

"I gather Denny refused," Tess said, "and he didn't want Lily to come, either. Lily did show up for the pageant meeting this afternoon, but otherwise she seems to be sticking close to home, at Denny's request."

"That doesn't sound like Denny."

"They're having a little problem communicating right now," Tess said.

"Because of what happened between Lily and Sherwood Draper?"

"Probably."

Mike frowned. "So, Denny finally got fed up with Lily's antics."

"It would seem so."

"Have you heard anything about Mavis Draper's trial?"

"I've talked to her several times since her arrest. I don't think the trial's scheduled yet. Between you and me, I'm not sure the police have enough evidence to convict her."

He looked down at her with a puzzled expression. "Why do you think that?"

"Because I was with Sherwood Draper when he died, and he was conscious and talking. But he didn't accuse Mavis."

"You told the police he said 'Nancy something.' Are you saying he also accused somebody of stabbing him?"

Tess shook her head. "No. What he said was 'Nancy Howard.' His sister's name was Nancy. She was killed in a car crash more than twenty years ago. At first, I wasn't sure he was saying his sister's name, because her last name wasn't Howard. But I got the old newspaper articles about Nancy's death, and it turns out the driver of the car, who was drunk, was named Howard. Howard Heisman. I think the professor was saying two names, not one. I just can't figure out what he meant to tell me about his sister and the man who killed her."

Mike was thoughtful for a moment. "Sounds like you're making a lot of assumptions to me, Tess."

"Maybe so. But Heisman was convicted of negligent homicide and given a twenty-year prison sentence. He ran away and has never been found."

He looked down at her with raised brows. "You've really been doing some digging. Why are you so interested in this?"

"I'm not convinced Mavis Draper killed her husband."

"The police know what they're doing, Tess. Besides, I don't see how it could be anyone else."

The police in this case being Andy Neill, Tess wasn't so sure. But she decided not to voice the idea that had popped into her mind earlier that day, as she read the newspaper articles for at least the dozenth time. What if

Professor Draper had learned something about Howard Heisman in Victoria Springs? Could she find out what and who had told him? If she voiced these questions, Mike might think she was crazy. Everybody probably would.

Instead, she said, "I hope so."

The song ended, and Mike danced her back to the table, bowing as he thanked her for the dance.

In that moment, she had another, even crazier thought.

Later that night, after Madison and Curt were in bed, Tess and Luke watched Jimmy Stewart in *It's a Wonderful Life* on TV.

Halfway through, Luke said sleepily, "Why are we watching this? I've seen it so many times I can say all the actors' lines."

"It's a tradition," Tess murmured. "The drama Claire found for the pageant is sort of an updated take-off on this story."

"Hmmm."

She lifted her head from Luke's shoulder to peer at him. His eyes were closed. "You asleep?"

"Just checking my eyelids for pinholes." He yawned and stretched, extending both arms in front of him.

Tess curled her legs up beneath her and rested her head on the back of the couch.

"Penny for your thoughts," Luke said.

"They're not worth it," Tess murmured.

"Try me."

Tess was still mulling over the crazy thought she'd had at the sock hop. "I was thinking about beards."

He blinked at her. "If you're going to suggest I grow one, forget it. I tried it once, and it was not a pretty sight."

"I prefer you clean-shaven, love."

"Good, because I've always had a suspicion that men who wear beards are hiding receding chins or some other defect." He bent to kiss her. "I'll never make it to the end of the movie. I'd better go home while I'm still alert enough to drive."

Tess couldn't keep her mind on the movie, either. After Luke left, she went to her office and studied the newspaper photograph of Howard Heisman.

She could see no resemblance to anyone involved in the Sherwood Draper case, most of whom she considered friends. She put the newspaper article aside, telling herself she was grasping at a very feeble straw.

Straw or not, she couldn't let go of it. Several times during the night, she woke up with an image of Sherwood Draper's face in her head, his pleading, dying eyes as he uttered his last words. He had been trying to tell her something about Howard Heisman, she was sure of it. If he had discovered Heisman's whereabouts, it must have happened on the day of his death, or surely he'd have mentioned it to his wife. Since Draper had spent most of the day at the church, it was logical to assume he'd learned something about Heisman there. This was borne out by the threatening note he'd written, telling somebody who had information, possibly about Heisman, to turn it over to the police.

Somebody. Or Heisman himself.

Could such an incredible coincidence have happened? Draper being invited to Victoria Springs because Lily Brookside had a crush on him and coming face to face with his sister's killer?

Anything was possible, Tess told herself as she finally gave up on sleep and crawled out of bed at 6 a.m.

She drank three cups of coffee and watched the "Today" show. Curt and Madison were still asleep when she finally decided to take action. She left a note for them on the kitchen table, saying she'd be back soon.

At the police station, no one was manning the desk, so she stuck her head in the chief's office where Andy Neill was having doughnuts and coffee.

He looked up and frowned. "Hey, Tess. Where'd you come from?"

"There was no one at the desk outside," she said apologetically. "So I came on in."

"McCorkle was there a minute ago." He didn't seem happy to see her. "Must be in the can."

"Do you have a few minutes?"

He licked sugary flakes of icing off his fingers and sat back in his chair, clearly enjoying his temporary occupation of the chief's office. His expression, however, was skeptical. "Only a few."

Tess remained standing and pulled the copies of the newspaper articles about Nancy Draper's death, and Howard Heisman's conviction and disappearance from her coat pocket. She tossed them to Neill. "Read," she said.

He read, or at least scanned them, then dropped them on the desk. "What's this got to do with anything?"

"Howard is the name of the man who was driving when Sherwood Draper's sister was killed."

"So?"

"Draper said 'Howard' before he died. I think he was trying to say Howard Heisman."

Neill glanced pointedly at his watch. "Look, Tess—"

"Let me finish, Andy. Please. I think Sherwood Draper saw Howard Heisman at the church and left that note in the overcoat pocket."

He crossed his arms. "Are you saying this Howard Heisman goes by some other name now, Tess?"

"Think about it, Andy. Heisman has been a fugitive for twenty years. Wouldn't it be easier to disappear if you took a new name?"

"Oh, for God's sake, Tess. That's so farfetched—wait a minute, you're not saying Bill Chandler is this Howard Heisman."

"No. Bill is almost ten years older than Howard Heisman would be today." She paused to think for a moment. "At least, he claims to be. And he looks it, too. Therefore, Draper put the note in the wrong coat for some reason I haven't figured out yet. Just let me finish."

Neill continued to sit, arms crossed, his face impassive, while Tess talked.

"If you would bring all the suspects together—" He opened his mouth and Tess held up her hand. "I know, as far as you're concerned Mavis Draper is the only suspect, but you asked for my cooperation, Andy. Now I'm asking for yours." She dug a list of names from her pocket and laid it on his desk. "Call these people and tell them to be at the church tomorrow afternoon at two. You might just leave there with the real murderer."

He looked at her for a long moment and then he picked up the list of names. "No, Tess. This isn't some Jessica Fletcher TV show." He handed her back the articles and the list of names. "Now, if you'll excuse me, I'm busy."

"Okay. Then I'll call these people together. I'll tell them it's for pageant practice. If you can take the time from your busy schedule, you're welcome to come. It's possible you'll learn something."

He grinned. "You know what, Tess? I'm beginning to understand why you bug the chief so much. You're worse than a bulldog with a bone. You just keep gnawing around on this, won't give it up. The bed and breakfast not keeping you busy or what?"

Tess didn't consider that worthy of response.

"Promise me something," Neill said.

"What?"

"If you end up with egg on your face Sunday afternoon, you'll give up this crazy notion that I've got the wrong person in custody."

Tess swallowed. "Agreed."

"Okay, now I've got work to do," he said in curt dismissal.

Egg on her face, huh? Tess thought as she drove home. She'd show Andy Neill! Her next thought was, Tess, you are about to make a fool of yourself in front of God and everybody.

It was her only chance to prove she was right, so she'd better come up with something more substantial than a few old newspaper articles. The problem was, she didn't have a clue what that something more might be.

Well . . . She squared her shoulders. She had more than twenty-four hours to figure it out.

*Chapter 20*

"Do you two have any plans for this afternoon?"
Tess asked. She, Curt, and Madison were having
lunch in her kitchen—lasagna, spinach salad, and
French bread.

"What are you going to do, Tess?" Madison
asked.

"There's a pageant practice at the church."

"Luke said I could come over and surf the net
again sometime," Curt said.

"Luke will be at practice today. You can come
with me if you want."

"Maybe I will."

"What about you, Madison?"

"I think I'll stay home and read my book. I'm
almost halfway through already."

Curt clapped his forehead, presumably panto-
miming one of the more flamboyant TV preachers.
"It's a miracle!" he cried.

Madison made a face at him. "Okay, Madison,"
Tess said. "Nedra will probably be here working
until four o'clock or so. I should be back by then."

After lunch, Tess retired to her office. She leafed
through the pageant play booklet until she found the
particular speech she wanted. Bill Chandler would
recite it in the Christmas drama in his role as the
father of two teenagers. After reading the passage,

she laid the booklet aside, shuffled through the newspaper articles from the Orono newspaper and found the one that mentioned Howard Heisman's mother. An idea of how to stage the gathering at church tomorrow afternoon was beginning to take shape.

Tess reached for the phone and dialed information. She asked for the number of Agnes Heisman in Bangor, Maine. After a few seconds, the operator said, "Please hold for that number."

Tess wrote the number down and hung up. She expelled a tense breath. Step one accomplished. If she hadn't been able to find a number for Agnes Heisman, her plan would have died on the drawing board.

She tucked the play booklet and a small tape recorder in her purse and left with Curt for the church.

The actors had read through the play once, while sitting in the front pew. Bill Chandler was the father; Lily Brookside, the mother; and Eddie Zoller and Brenda Brookside, the teenage children. It was a story about a father who'd lost his job two weeks before Christmas and had to tell his family there was no money for Christmas presents, not even for a tree. But the mother had insisted they didn't need money to have a wonderful Christmas. The remainder of the play showed how they accomplished that, and, of course, it turned out to be the best Christmas they'd ever had and everybody learned that love and family were more important than material things.

"Let's take a ten-minute break," Claire said, "and then we'll go through it again on stage."

Tess grabbed Bill Chandler in the foyer. "I need you to do me a huge favor," she said. "Tell Claire you've got a scratchy throat and have to rest your voice." Then she told him who she wanted to take his place for the next reading.

He looked at her blankly.

"I'll explain everything later," Tess urged. "Please just do it, Bill."

He shrugged and muttered, "Whatever," in that tone men use when they are humoring a woman.

"Thank you," Tess said and returned to the sanctuary. Tess hadn't had to put much pressure on Claire to call another practice Sunday afternoon at two. Claire agreed they needed all the practice they could get, since they'd had such a late start. Tess hadn't told Claire the real reason she wanted a Sunday afternoon session.

Now for the next step in the plan.

When the players reconvened in the sanctuary, Claire went along with the switch in players. Tess pulled out her tape recorder. "I'm going to record it this time so you all can hear yourselves tomorrow. Nothing like hearing yourself on tape to pick out where you need to work on your delivery."

Claire and Bill exchanged a puzzled look, and Claire turned to contemplate Tess for an instant. Even Luke, who had a very minor part in the play, lifted a quizzical brow.

Tess gave him a smile and placed the tape recorder at the edge of the stage. She tensed when the players reached the crucial passage, where the father talks about what a dismal Christmas it will be without money and how he doesn't deserve what's happened to him. Later, when Tess, Luke, and Curt left the church together, Luke asked, "Anybody want to stop for ice cream?"

"Yeah!" Curt said.

Tess grinned at Luke. "Silly question."

Tess drove away from the church and headed for the ice cream parlor. They were in her car, as Luke's Jag didn't accommodate more than two people comfortably.

"Can I have a hot fudge sundae?" Curt asked from the back seat.

"Whatever your little heart desires," Luke said, with a glance at Tess. "Unless Tess is afraid you'll ruin your dinner."

Tess laughed. "I'm not too worried about that. And, before I forget, Luke, could we go by your house on the way home? I need to borrow your tape recorder."

"Sure," Luke agreed, "but what's wrong with yours?"

"Nothing. I just want to have a backup."

Luke gave her a skeptical look. "You've already taped the play, sweetheart. What are you really up to?"

She batted her eyes at him. "Up to?"

"I know that look."

She couldn't maintain the innocent pose, not with Luke. "All will be made clear in due time, dear," she promised.

Curt leaned over the back seat between them. "Tess, can we get some more of that chocolate chip ice cream? Last night, I emptied the carton you had in your freezer."

Tess assured him that they'd get another half-gallon.

Tess closeted herself in her office as soon as they returned to Iris House, telling Curt and Madison that she had work to do. After putting a fresh tape in Luke's recorder, she played back the drama she'd taped at church until she found the one brief speech she wanted. She recorded that speech on the new tape.

Then she rewound the new tape and played it back. Luke's machine was state-of-the-art, and the speaker's voice came across loud and clear. Tess hoped it would also be recognizable to the person who would be listening on the other end of the phone.

Howard Heisman had been driving his mother's car when he disappeared. He'd abandoned it soon after his disappearance, but he'd risked a phone call to tell her where she could find it.

It was conceivable—no, likely, Tess told herself—that he'd made other phone calls through the years. Not to tell Agnes where he was, but to assure her that he was all right.

Now, if only she could reach Heisman's mother. Tess went to the phone and dialed the number she'd written down yesterday. A woman answered.

"I have a long-distance call for Agnes Heisman," Tess said.

"This is Agnes."

"One moment please." Tess held the receiver over the two tape machines. One would play the message she'd prepared, the other would record it and Agnes Heisman's response.

Tess punched the appropriate buttons.

# Chapter 21

Potted poinsettias, placed around the base of the raised platform at the front of the sanctuary, formed a red semicircle. A beautiful wreath of evergreen boughs and red velvet ribbons decorated the podium used by the pastor during the Sunday morning service. Somebody had moved the podium to one side for pageant practice. Large red velvet bows also decorated the ends of the pews.

All very festive.

Tess felt anything but festive as she clasped her tape player and scanned the audience.

Bill Chandler and Denny Brookside were helping Claire move some of the chairs the choir had used that morning to make room for the actors. Bill and Claire looked more relaxed today than they'd been since the murder. Not so Denny. Deep lines bracketed his mouth.

Denny had no role in the pageant, and Tess hadn't been sure he'd come. But apparently, since Lily refused to drop out of the pageant, he'd come to keep an eye on her. Even so, he seemed to be avoiding any conversation with his wife.

Lily, who was playing the mother in the drama, sat in the front pew, silently going over her lines. As were Luke and Pam Yoder, the two others who had parts in the drama.

185

Elizabeth Purcell, the organist, and Mike Tandy, as well as a few other choir members were present, too. The choir was scheduled to practice at three-thirty.

Madison and Curt were seated with the Brookside twins and Eddie Zoller in the second pew.

Blanche Tandy sat on Tess's left. "I think the pageant is going to be okay," she said as she sat down. "For a while there, I was worried we wouldn't pull one together this year."

Tess had nodded in agreement and had momentarily considered abandoning her plan. But remembering Mavis Draper, she couldn't.

Claire spoke, snagging Tess's attention. "That'll do for now," Claire said, motioning Bill and Mike from the stage. "Let's do a read-through first, and then we'll see how well we can do without scripts." She glanced toward the back of the sanctuary and stiffened.

Tess turned around. Andy Neill had entered the sanctuary and slipped quietly into a back pew.

Tess cleared her throat and stood. "Claire, I'd like to play the tape first."

Claire glanced at Tess, then back at Andy Neill. "Did you want to talk to us, Officer Neill?"

All heads turned toward the back of the sanctuary. Expressions ranged from mild curiosity to clear wariness.

"Not right now," Neill said. "I was just passing by and saw all the cars. Thought I'd see how practice was going." He looked at Tess. "You all go ahead with what you were doing." Clearly a lie, and everybody knew it. What they didn't know was that he'd come hoping to see Tess with egg on her face.

Bill glanced from his wife to Tess to Neill, his gaze cold and measuring.

"I'm sure your time is too valuable to sit through our pageant practice, Officer Neill," Claire said. She was clearly flustered.

"Don't worry about it," Neill muttered, still watching Tess.

"Well—" Claire darted a look at her husband. "Let's get started then. Tess, we're pressed for time. We'll hear the tape later."

Tess leaned over a poinsettia plant and set the tape machine on the stage. "I really think we should do it now, Claire."

Claire raked a hand through her hair. She was plainly prepared to argue. "Tess—"

"Oh, for God's sake!" Lily Brookside exploded. "Let her play the tape and get it over with."

Claire glared at Lily, started to protest, then changed her mind. She walked to a pew and sat down. "Go ahead," she sighed with a wave of her hand.

Tess had stationed herself where she could see everybody in the audience. She punched the play button and clasped her hands together tightly at her waist.

A man's voice issued from the tape. "It's the worst Christmas ever. I've tried to live an upright life—"

Lily Brookside's play booklet rustled. "You didn't rewind it all the way, Tess."

"Yes, start at the beginning," Pam Yoder said.

Tess stopped the tape and rewound it to the beginning of the father's speech. "Just bear with me, please. This'll only take a few moments." She started the tape again and watched the man whose voice issued from the machine, the man who had taken Bill Chandler's place in yesterday's practice.

"It's the worst Christmas ever. I've tried to live an upright life, but everything's falling apart. I feel like I've let the family down. What have I done to deserve this?"

There was a pause and then an unfamiliar woman's voice wailed, "Howard? Oh, Howard, I've been so worried about you. It's been so long since you called. What's happened, son?"

Claire had been sitting, chin cupped in her hand, the diamonds in her wedding band reflecting sparks of light. Now she straightened, frowning at Tess. "Who's *that*?"

Denny Brookside finally looked at his wife. Lily lifted

her hands in a don't-ask-me gesture. "That's not in the play, Tess," Lily said.

Brenda Brookside's eyes glittered with curiosity. "Yeah, what's going on?"

Luke and Curt watched Tess with expressions of amazement.

Eddie Zoller bowed his head, rubbing a hand over his short-clipped hair.

Blanche Tandy's lips parted as she sent her husband a bewildered look.

Tess took them all in at a quick glance before returning her gaze to Mike Tandy, whose expression had gone from boredom to intent alertness as he listened to the woman on the tape. Now, he might have been carved from stone.

"Before Sherwood Draper died," Tess began, "he said two names. One name was Nancy, his younger sister, who died in a car with a drunk driver at the wheel in 1976. The driver was convicted of negligent homicide, but disappeared before he could be imprisoned. He has never been apprehended. That man's name was Howard—Howard Heisman. And the second name Sherwood Draper said was Howard. You heard the woman on the tape, Agnes Heisman—Howard's mother—identify the other speaker as Howard."

There was a stunned silence. Then Blanche Tandy said, "But that was Mike on the tape." Her voice shook. "This is insane."

"I'm sorry, Blanche," Tess said, glancing at Mike, who continued to sit like a statue in the pew. "But there is a way Mike can prove right away that he isn't Howard Heisman."

"How?" It was Blanche, not Mike, who asked the question.

"By shaving off his beard," Tess said. It was Luke's remark about men wearing beards to hide defects that had convinced Tess that one particular crazy idea of hers wasn't so crazy, after all. "Howard Heisman has a two-inch scar on his chin from a childhood accident." Heisman's fingerprints would be on file in Maine, too, of course, but Tess wanted to give Mike a chance to clear himself here and now. She wanted desperately to be proved wrong.

Blanche took a shaky breath. "All right then, that's what he'll do." Mike said nothing. "Right, Mike?" No response.

Lily Brookside's voice was indulgent and faintly amused. "I swear, Tess, you get the most outlandish ideas. If what you're saying is true, I assume that woman on the tape hasn't seen her son in more than twenty years. It was clever of you to tape Mike delivering that particular speech, by the way, and then play it over the phone for Agnes Heisman. That is what you did, isn't it?" She didn't wait for Tess's reply. "But you heard her say she hadn't heard from her son in ages. She's probably so desperate to hear from him that she would identify almost any male voice saying those words on the phone as her son."

"Lily's right, Tess," Denny put in. "Where did you get the notion that Mike is this Heisman fellow?"

"It came to me Friday night," Tess said, "at the teen sock hop. Before that, for a little while I thought it might be Bill Chandler."

"Now, look here, Tess—" Bill sputtered.

"Only because of Sherwood Draper's note, Bill," Tess said hastily. "You've all heard about the note Bill found in his overcoat pocket. It said that the recipient had twenty-four hours to 'do the right thing' or Draper would go to the police. I don't know how it got in Bill's coat pocket. Maybe Draper mistook his coat for Howard Heisman's. But, however it got there, it confirmed my suspicion that Mavis Draper didn't kill her husband. The murderer was somebody Draper recognized from the past, somebody who had information the police would be interested in. Once I found the articles about Nancy Draper's death, and the conviction and disappearance of the driver of the car, I began to suspect that Draper had seen somebody he recognized as Howard Heisman that day at the church. Then, he'd written the note, giving Heisman twenty-four hours to turn himself in. That's what Draper was trying to tell me. Unfortunately, all he was able to say before he died was his sister's name and the name of her killer.''

As Tess spoke, Andy Neill had come quietly down the aisle, but nobody else seemed to notice. All eyes were on Tess.

Claire Chandler spoke. "My God, Tess, you're saying that Mike Tandy is this Howard Heisman, and that Draper recognized him and threatened to expose him.''

Tess nodded unhappily. She looked at Mike. "I don't know what happened, but I suspect there was a confrontation between Draper and the man he threatened, which ended in Draper's death.''

Blanche shot to her feet. "Wait just a damned minute here, Tess Darcy. If that note was in Bill's coat, how did Mike even know about it?''

This was one aspect of the scenario that Tess hadn't figured out. "I don't know, Blanche. Bill threw the note into the waste basket in the church foyer, which is where I found it later. Maybe Mike saw the note before I took it out of the basket.''

"I'll never forgive you for this, Tess. You've lost your mind!'' Blanche flared. "This is all too ludicrous to believe.''

"Easy to prove her wrong,'' Andy Neill said. Everybody turned to stare at him. Everybody except Mike Tandy. "Mike, would you come with me, please. We'll find a razor and settle this once and for all.''

For a long moment, Mike just sat mutely, staring down at his knees.

Blanche slowly, pleadingly reached out toward him.

Mike cleared his throat. "That won't be necessary, Officer Neill. I am—was Howard Heisman . . . in another lifetime. But I didn't kill Sherwood Draper.''

# Chapter 22

Mike Tandy definitely had the audience's full attention.

"Mike, what are you saying?" Blanche cried.

"I'm so sorry, honey," he said miserably, "but it's all going to come out now."

"*What's* going to come out?"

"I'm sorry," he said again. "Maybe I should have told you years ago, but I hoped you'd never have to know."

Blanche sagged into the pew and began to cry silently.

Mike stood slowly and walked to where Andy Neill stood in the aisle. "I put that note in Bill's pocket."

"Well, thanks a lot!" Bill sputtered.

"I didn't know it was your coat at the time, Bill," Mike said miserably. "I didn't know *whose* coat it was. But I was alone in the foyer when I found the note in *my* coat pocket. As I was reading it, I heard somebody coming. I guess I panicked and stuck it in the nearest pocket."

"The note wasn't signed," Neill said. "Did you know who'd written it?"

"Oh, yeah. I think, down deep, I've been expecting something like that for twenty years. I knew who Draper was the first time I heard his name Friday morning. I wanted to leave the church right then, before he saw me, but I didn't know how to explain that to Blanche—and everybody. I was afraid it would raise too many questions. And I told myself my appearance had changed so much since '76 that Draper wouldn't recognize me. I've gained a lot of weight and—'' He stroked his beard. ''Grew this beard and moustache. I decided to stay and keep away from Draper as much as possible.''

Claire, who'd been listening raptly, suddenly blurted, ''That's why you kept that sweatshirt hood pulled down to your eyes. You were afraid he'd recognize you. And the Santa suit! The powder in your beard and moustache! The glasses! I've been wondering why you wanted to come to practice in that costume. It was a disguise!''

''That's right, Claire, but it didn't work. I noticed Draper staring at me a couple of times after lunch, and then I found that note . . .'' He lifted both hands and let them drop in a helpless gesture. ''As soon as I read it, while the choir was taking a break, I went backstage to talk to Draper. I told him how sorry I was about his sister and about running away. I said I'd lived a good life for more than twenty years and I had a wife who knew nothing about my past. I told him it wasn't just my life he wanted to destroy. It was Blanche's, too. I begged him not to go to the police.''

''But he refused,'' Neill said sharply, ''so you picked up those shears and stabbed him.''

Mike was shaking his head adamantly. ''No! No, that's not what happened. Draper went into a rage and swore I'd pay for what I'd done to his sister. He was yelling so loud, I was sure somebody would hear him. I realized I was wasting my time, trying to talk to him, so I left the dressing room. I didn't see anybody backstage, so I guessed nobody heard him, after all.''

''You're trying to tell us you walked out and left him alive?'' Neill asked disbelievingly. ''Knowing he'd go to the police.''

''I swear he was alive when I left him,'' Mike said. He

gripped the end of the pew with one hand, as if to steady himself. "I was going to call you, Neill, after practice that day and turn myself in. After I'd told Blanche everything. I'm too old and too tired to run again." He glanced at his wife, who still sat with her head bowed, one hand over her eyes. "Besides, I couldn't walk out on Blanche with no explanation. She—she's my life." He stared at his wife, as if willing her to look at him, but she didn't. He looked back at Neill. "Then Draper was killed, so I kept quiet."

"Mighty convenient for you," Neill snarled, "him dying when he did."

Mike hung his head. "I don't deny that."

"Way too convenient!" Neill snapped. "Meanwhile, you let me arrest Draper's wife for what you did!"

"I swear—"

"You can tell it to a jury," Neill interrupted. He grabbed the handcuffs that dangled from his belt. "Mike Tandy, I am arresting you for the murder of Sherwood Draper. You have the right to remain silent. If you choose not to exercise that right, whatever you say can and will be used against you in a court of law. You have the right to an attorney—"

"*Stop!*" Eddie Zoller leaped from his seat and ran out into the aisle. "Mike didn't do it! I did."

There were gasps and murmurs from all directions and half the audience was on its feet now. Tess heard Brenda Boyd wail, "No, Eddie!" Blanche, who had finally composed herself, though her face was as pale as death, got up and went to where Mike and Eddie stood. She clasped Mike's hand, placing her other hand on Eddie's shoulder. "I know you want to help Mike, Eddie, but you can't do this."

"She's right, Eddie," Mike said. "We just have to trust the police to find the real killer."

"But I did kill him, Mike. It's tearing me up. I almost told you a couple of times, but—you acted like you—didn't want to talk to me, like you were mad at me."

"Aw, Eddie, I was never mad at you, I just had a lot on my mind."

"Eddie, honey—" Blanche began.

Neill raised his voice. "Let the boy talk! Go ahead, Eddie."

"Mike, you said nobody heard Draper yelling at you backstage, but I did. I went backstage looking for you while you were in the dressing room with him. He was accusing Mike of killing his sister and threatening him. I heard Mike coming out of the dressing room and ran and hid behind the curtain. Then I went in and tried to talk to Draper." He looked at Neill, "I just wanted to tell him what a good person Mike is." Eddie's voice broke.

Blanche put her arm around him. "Oh, Eddie . . ."

Sobs tore from the boy's chest. Several moments passed before he could control himself. Then he wiped tears from his eyes. "Draper told me to get out, that he was going to make sure Mike spent the rest of his life in prison, and he—he shoved me toward the door and turned his back—and I—I saw the shears on the couch and I grabbed them. All I could think of was that I had to keep him from hurting Mike. So I—I stabbed him. He fell and there was all that blood. I couldn't believe what I'd done. Now I know he wasn't dead yet, but I thought he was then. And I—I couldn't believe I'd killed him. I wiped my fingerprints off the shears and left him. Then I ran out of there. Nobody was backstage when I came out. Nobody saw me."

Blanche turned away and began to cry again, her face buried in Mike's chest, as he embraced her with one arm. Neill had already clamped the cuffs on his other wrist.

"We'll sort this out at the station," Neill said. He cuffed Eddie to Mike.

"Blanche, call a lawyer," Mike said.

Tess watched Neill lead his prisoners away, while visualizing the scene Eddie had described. Draper turning his back contemptuously on Eddie as the boy noticed the shears lying on the sofa. Eddie, hardly thinking about what he was doing, thinking only of protecting Mike. Eddie grabbing the shears and stabbing Draper.

Yet Draper hadn't named Eddie as he died. Instead, he had named his sister's killer, as though identifying the man who'd gotten away with murdering Nancy was weighing more heavily on his mind than naming the boy who'd stabbed him.

Claire wisely cancelled the pageant practice.

*Chapter 23*

It was Christmas night and Tess made one last trip through the guest parlor, picking up coffee cups and dessert plates. With the entire Darcy family together at Iris House, it had been the best Christmas she could remember. Even the pageant on the twenty-first had turned out pretty well, in spite of the fact that everybody was still in shock over Mike's being unmasked as Howard Heisman and Eddie Zoller's confessing to the murder of Sherwood Draper. It was after eleven now and all the presents, but one, had been opened and exclaimed over. The remaining gift was for Blanche Tandy. Tess would take it to her tomorrow, as a sort of peace offering, if Blanche would let her in the door.

The Forrests and Cody Yount had gone home, and Tess's family had retired, her father and Zelda to the Darcy Flame suite, which had been vacated by Mavis Draper the day she was released from jail, all charges against her dropped. The last time Tess saw Luke, he had fallen asleep on the couch in her apartment sitting room.

She carried the few dirty dishes to the kitchen and put them in the dishwasher, which was already full for the third time that day. She added detergent, punched the "wash" button, and wandered back through the dining room to the parlor. In a corner of the velvet settee, she noticed the Carolyn Hart mystery Madison had finished that afternoon. Madison had even asked her mother to buy her another Hart mystery at Cinny's bookshop for her to read on the flight home. Zelda had proclaimed Tess a miracle worker.

Tess picked up the book and carried it to her apartment. She'd return it to the library tomorrow.

As she entered the sitting room quietly, Luke stirred and opened one eye to peer at her.

"I fell asleep," he mumbled, rubbing his hands over his face.

Tess laid the book on the side table next to the blue chair where Primrose dozed. "I noticed."

"Where've you been?"

"Picking up the last of the dishes."

Luke sat up and patted the cushion beside him. "Sit down and relax. You've had a long day."

"A wonderful day," Tess sighed as Luke pulled her into the crook of his arm. Then she added, "Considering," as she thought of what Blanche Tandy was going through.

He kissed the top of her head. "Zelda swears you hypnotized Madison to get her to read that book and ask for another."

"I knew if I could get her to read the first few pages, she'd finish it," Tess said. "Good mysteries always hook you fast."

"Speaking of mysteries," Luke said, "somebody ought to write about Sherwood Draper's murder and all that led up to it."

"There's a crime reporter on the Orono newspaper who will. I promised to call him if Professor Draper's murder turned out to be connected to his sister's death. I'll do that next week.

"Can you imagine," she went on, "how awful it must have been for Mike, living for more than twenty years with the fear that someone somewhere would recognize him as an escaped criminal?"

"No, I can't. I wonder how Blanche is holding up."

Tess let her head drop to his shoulder. "I don't know. I'm going to stop by her place tomorrow and see if she'll talk to me, since I was the one to expose Mike publicly. She did say she'd never forgive me."

"She's got so many other things to deal with right now, I doubt she'll have the energy to hold a grudge."

"Poor Blanche. But they'll get through it. According to Cody, with time off for good behavior, Mike could be out in five or six years. It's Eddie who may spend the rest of his life behind bars. Neill wants to charge him as an adult." Like Blanche, Tess had not fully believed Eddie's confession, knowing he'd do anything to protect Mike. She'd half-expected him to recant the confession once he'd had time to think it over.

It hadn't happened.

After Neill turned out to be the one with egg on his face for arresting Mavis Draper, he'd set out to make certain he had the right person this time. Tess had talked to him once since he'd arrested Mike and Eddie. He'd merely said the investigation was continuing. But yesterday, he'd returned Mike to Maine to face the charges there, which had to mean he no longer considered Mike a suspect in Draper's murder.

Pulling her mind away from those sad thoughts, Tess nestled more comfortably against Luke's shoulder. The day had been a success. The breakfast coffee cake and finger foods, prepared earlier by Gertie, frozen until needed, had been delicious. Dinner, with the help of Dahlia and Zelda, not to mention Gertie's recipes, was perfect. Like everybody else, Tess had overeaten, and now that she could finally relax, weariness dragged at her. She closed her eyes.

The phone rang.

Tess groaned. "Who could that be at this hour?"

"Want me to get it?"

"No." Tess reached for the phone which sat on the

small secretary, grabbing the receiver off the hook before it could ring again.

She cleared her throat. "Hello."

"Hope I didn't wake you, Tess." It was Andy Neill. "I drove by your house and saw your lights on. Figured you were still up."

"I'm up, Andy. And why are you driving around after 11 p.m. on Christmas night?"

"Had to take over for the officer who was scheduled for tonight's patrol. He called in sick. Too much turkey and dressing, I guess."

"I know the feeling," Tess said. "What's up, Andy?"

"We got hard evidence against Eddie Zoller. Thought you'd want to know."

Tess sighed. "I don't know whether to be sad for Eddie or glad for Mike."

"Know what you mean. Anyway, the scene-of-crime guys found fibers in that dressing room that match the sweater Eddie was wearing that day. Unless his lawyer can prove he was in there at some other time . . ."

"I doubt that he was," Tess said. "He would have had no reason to be."

"We got a fingerprint match, too. He's saying now that he doesn't remember much of those few minutes, he panicked and things went black. The fact that he wiped his prints off the handles of those shears makes it look otherwise. The tech picked up Eddie's prints on the inside of the door facing."

"Sounds like you've got a solid case this time."

"Well, you never know what a jury will do. Blanche Tandy hired a hotshot lawyer to defend him, if you can believe it. He's sure to bring up Eddie's pitiful past, dead mother, abusive father, all that." He paused. "Uh, Tess, I wanted to thank you. That little drama you staged at the church saved me from making an even bigger fool of myself than I already had. I—uh—well, the chief's due back next week. He knows Mavis Draper's been released and that I've made another arrest, but he hasn't heard—well, all the details yet."

Tess thought she knew what was worrying him, why he'd called to give her the news about Eddie. It wasn't to keep her informed. Neill wanted to cover his butt, and he wanted her to help him. "As far as I'm concerned, Chief Butts doesn't need to know that gathering was totally my idea. You were there, too, Andy. Against your better judgment, but you came." To watch her make a fool of herself, she thought but didn't say. "You could tell the chief it was a cooperative effort."

She heard Neill release a long breath. "Yeah, I could. I appreciate this, Tess. I really do."

"Don't mention it, Andy," Tess said, before hanging up.

"Sounded like he's worried Butts will rake him over the coals for arresting the wrong person," Luke said as Tess returned to his side.

"Knowing Butts, he's probably right to be concerned."

"And Neill wants to say he was a major force in tracking down the real killer?"

"Something like that. It doesn't matter to me. Butts wouldn't congratulate me if he knew I was behind Mike's and Eddie's arrests. He'd just raise the roof because I'd stuck my nose into police business."

"It's Butts's nature to complain about something."

"I know." She turned her head to press her lips against his cheek. "I'm worn out, honey. I need to get some sleep."

"Me, too," he said, but he didn't move. "But first, there's one more present you can give me."

She sent him a questioning look. They'd already exchanged their gifts. She'd given him a beautiful lambswool sweater, the most expensive set of Polo toiletries she could find, and a leather-bound organizer for business use. "You're going to have to give me another one, too," she said finally. "I want several hours of your time. You'll have to teach me how to use my new toy." Tess's present from Luke had been a notebook computer. After a brief moment of disappointment that it wasn't something more romantic, she'd been thrilled with it.

"Done," he said.

"Now, what else can I give you?"

"A yes."

"What?"

"I've been trying to say something for days, but it never seemed the right time. I love you desperately, Tess Darcy."

She threw her arms around his neck. "I love you, too."

"Then, what are we waiting for? Will you marry me?"

"Oh, Luke . . ." She hugged him even tighter and buried her face in his neck. She had known this moment was coming, sooner or later. Still, her head swam and her stomach turned over, a combination of happiness and fear. Luke had mentioned marriage several times in the past in round-about sorts of ways, but he'd never come right out with a proposal before. And she did love him. With all her heart. Only . . .

When she didn't speak, he said, "I know what you're doing. You're thinking of all the reasons why you can't say yes."

"It's just—" She lifted her head to look into his blue eyes. "This apartment isn't really big enough for the two of us, but I can't leave Iris House, Luke. I have to be on the premises, available to my guests. And I couldn't ask you to leave your house because you have that wonderful office there and—"

He placed two fingers over her mouth to stop her words. "Details, sweetheart. We can work it out. We don't even have to set a date right away. All I want from you now is a yes."

"*Right* now?"

His steady blue gaze, so full of love, was also determined. But he relented a little. "You can have one day—okay, two days—to think it over, Tess. Then I want your answer."

\* \* \*

The next afternoon, Tess went to the Tandy house, a neat white cottage with green shutters and a white picket fence. When Mike and Blanche bought it, it had been in deplorable condition. Restoring it had been a labor of love. Now Blanche was there alone. It must be a house full of memories that brought more pain than joy.

Tess's knock was answered by a Blanche she hardly recognized.

"Oh. It's you, Tess." In the past two weeks, she'd lost weight, and her facial skin sagged on the bones. She had aged ten years in appearance since Mike's arrest.

"May I come in for a minute, Blanche?"

She hesitated only momentarily. Tess sensed that even a minor confrontation was too much for Blanche at the moment. She ushered Tess in, and Tess set the gift she carried on the cherry coffee table.

"For me?" Blanche asked.

Tess nodded. "It's just a box of pretty stationery I found at Cinny's bookshop. It reminded me of you. Actually, it's a peace offering, Blanche. I know you're unhappy about the way I staged that little drama at the church in front of all your friends."

She sighed and gestured for Tess to sit on the couch, while she took a jade-colored side chair. "I was angry with you for a while, but I've realized that everybody would have known, eventually, no matter how you did it."

"Maybe I should have faced Mike in private, but at the time it seemed the best way. I'm sorry if I've caused you pain, Blanche."

She shrugged. "That's only a pin prick compared to the other pain I've endured."

"I know, dear. What can I do to help?"

"There's nothing anyone can do, Tess. They've taken Mike to Maine."

"I heard that."

"And Eddie will be tried for Sherwood Draper's murder."

"I know."

She shook her head. "He couldn't stand hearing Draper threaten Mike. In a crisis, he reverted to the violence he lived with before he came to us." Tears filled her eyes. "I've come to love that boy, Tess. The thought of him spending the rest of his life in prison just about kills me."

"I'm so sorry, Blanche. How is Mike holding up?"

"He keeps saying he let me down but, you know, I think he's actually relieved to have it all out in the open."

Not for the first time, Tess wondered how Mike had lived with the secret guilt of what he'd done all these years.

"All during our marriage, he let me think he had no family, and that he was from Iowa."

"Why Iowa?"

"Because after he ran away from Orono, he ended up in Iowa. That's where he became Mike Tandy. He found the name on the tombstone of a child born the same year as he, but who'd died at age three. He sent for the child's birth certificate and became Mike Tandy."

Tess had read of people doing that, of course. How easy it was to assume someone else's identity.

"He contacted his mother every year or so," Blanche went on, "but he never told her where he was. I've talked to her on the phone several times since Mike's arrest, and she wants me to come and visit her."

"The change of scenery would do you good," Tess said.

"You know, Mike always refused to consider adopting a baby. I thought it was because his own childhood was unhappy but, of course, he didn't want to undergo the background check. It's strange, but it's almost harder for me to forgive him for that than any of the other. I wanted a baby so desperately." Her voice broke and she looked at her hands clasped in her lap. She cleared her throat. "Mike was just an immature college kid when Nancy

Draper was killed, and when he realized he was going to prison, he panicked and ran. That I can understand.''

"Will you go to see Mike's mother soon?"

She nodded. ''I'm going to sell the house and move to whatever town is closest to where Mike will be.'' She looked thoughtful for a moment. ''His mother calls him Howard, of course, but I'm not used to thinking of him as Howard yet.''

"Blanche, you're going through a lot of emotional turmoil. It may not be the best time to make major decisions. Are you sure you want to sell the house?''

"Absolutely,'' she said emphatically. ''What's a house compared to Mike? You know, I've always given lip service to the idea that people are more important than things. Now I understand how true that is. I'll find a job in Maine, get to know his mother, and visit Mike as often as possible. It's odd, but in spite of what he's done, I love him now more than ever. At church that day, he said I was his life. Well, he's mine, too. Nothing is as important as that.'' Blanche looked around at her painstakingly decorated and furnished living room. She and Mike had hung the wallpaper and stripped and painted the woodwork. They'd done it together, and now that Mike was no longer there, it couldn't possibly give her the satisfaction it once had. Blanche took a deep breath. ''I'll call a realtor tomorrow and start packing.''

"Can I help with the packing?''

"That's sweet of you, Tess. I may just take you up on it.''

"Good. Now I need to get back to my family. You try to get some rest.''

They stood and came together in a spontaneous embrace. Blanche's arms tightened convulsively. ''Thanks for coming by, Tess,'' Blanche said brokenly, bringing tears to Tess's eyes. ''Not many people have.''

Driving back to Iris House, Tess continued to fight tears. Blanche was a strong woman. She would survive, and she and Mike would be together again some day. In five years or so, if Cody Yount was right.

*Nothing is as important as love*, Blanche had said. And she was right. Apparently Denny Brookside had reached that conclusion, too, for Lily had told Tess last week that she and Denny were talking again and even planning a second honeymoon.

*What's a house compared to Mike?* Blanche had asked.

Sometimes it took tragedy to help people put things in proper perspective. Sometimes it took a good friend saying the words.

Tess thought of Iris House and how much she loved it. But she loved Luke more. They could work out the details, he'd said. She knew it was true, even though she didn't know how at the moment.

But she did know now what her answer to Luke's proposal would be. And she couldn't wait to tell him.

She made a U-turn at the next corner and headed for Luke's house.

*Iris House Recipes*

## CHRISTMAS MORNING CRANBERRY COFFEE CAKE

*1 package active dry yeast*
*½ teaspoon ground nutmeg*
*About 3¼ cups all-purpose flour*
*⅔ cup milk*
*⅓ cup sugar*
*¼ cup butter or margarine*
*½ teaspoon salt*
*1 egg*
*1¼ cups cranberries*
*⅓ cup sugar*
*1 tablespoon water*
*1½ teaspoons finely shredded orange peel*
*½ teaspoon ground cinnamon*
*1 cup sifted powdered sugar*
*4 teaspoons milk*
*¼ teaspoon orange extract*

In a bowl, combine yeast, nutmeg, and 1¼ cups of the flour. In a saucepan, heat ⅔ cup milk, sugar, butter, and salt till warm and butter is almost melted, stirring constantly. Add to flour mixture. Add egg. Beat with electric mixer on low speed 30 seconds, scraping sides of bowl. Beat on high speed for 3 minutes. With a spoon, stir in as much of the remaining flour as you can. Turn out on a floured surface. Knead in enough remaining flour to make a moderately soft dough that is smooth and elastic. Shape into a ball. Place in a greased bowl, turn

once. Cover and let rise in a warm place till double in size (about 1 to 1¼ hours).

In a saucepan combine cranberries, sugar, water, orange peel, and cinnamon. Cook and stir over medium heat till berries pop. Cook and stir 3 minutes more till very thick. Cover and cool the mixture.

Punch dough down, cover, and let rest 10 minutes. On a lightly floured surface, roll dough into an 18×9–inch rectangle. Spread with cranberry filling. Roll up jelly-roll style from long side. Seal edges.

On a greased baking sheet shape in a ring; pinch to seal ends together. With kitchen shears, make cuts from outer edge almost to the center, making 12 pieces. Gently pull sections apart and twist dough on its side, overlapping slightly, to make a ring. Cover and let rise till nearly double in size (about 30 minutes).

Bake in a 375-degree oven for 20 to 25 minutes, covering with foil the last 10 minutes to prevent burning. Cool slightly on wire rack before glazing.

For glaze, combine powdered sugar, 4 teaspoons milk, and orange extract. Drizzle over ring. Makes 12 servings.

# DEEP FRIED TURKEY

*12–15 pound turkey*
*3 gallons peanut oil*
*Cooking pot large enough to accommodate turkey and oil*
*20 cc's onion juice*
*20 cc's garlic juice*
*Cayenne pepper*
*Large disposable hypodermic syringe with cubic centimeters (cc's) marked on side*
*3-inch, 18-gauge hypodermic needle*

Remove giblets from thawed turkey. Dry turkey with paper towels. Using the hypodermic syringe and the hypodermic needle, inject turkey all over with 20 cc's of onion juice and 20 cc's of garlic juice. Liberally sprinkle turkey with cayenne pepper.

Pour peanut oil into pot. There should be at least 8 inches between the oil and the rim of the pot. Heat oil to 350 degrees. (Use a thermometer with a hook that will hang over rim of pot.)

Tie turkey's legs together with wire or strong cord, leaving length enough to remove turkey from pot when done.

Holding the cord, lower the turkey into the heated oil. Cook at between 300 and 350 degrees, 4½ minutes per pound. Remove turkey, carve, and serve.

# CHRISTMAS FRUIT BREAD

*2¼ cups all-purpose flour*
*1½ cups sugar*
*1 cup butter or margarine, softened*
*1 8-ounce package cream cheese, softened*
*4 eggs*
*1½ teaspoons baking powder*
*1 teaspoon salt*
*1½ teaspoons vanilla extract*
*¾ cup candied red and/or green cherries, quartered*

*½ cup candied pineapple bits*
*½ cup chopped dates*
*½ cup golden raisins*
*½ cup chopped walnuts*

Heat oven to 325 degrees. In large bowl, combine 1¼ cups flour, sugar, butter, cream cheese, eggs, baking powder, salt, and vanilla. Beat with electric mixer at medium speed, scraping bowl often, until well mixed. By hand, stir in remaining 1 cup flour, candied cherries, candied pineapple, dates, raisins and walnuts. Pour into 6 greased 5½×3–inch mini loaf pans. Bake 45–55 minutes or until toothpick inserted in center comes out clean. Cool 10 minutes. Remove from pans. Cool completely

# SWEET POTATO CASSEROLE

*3¼ lbs. sweet potatoes*
*⅓ cup firmly packed brown sugar*
*⅓ cup unsweetened orange juice*
*¼ cup egg substitute*
*1½ teaspoons pumpkin pie spice*
*1 teaspoon butter flavoring*
*1 teaspoon grated orange peel*
*¼ teaspoon salt*
*Vegetable cooking spray*
*¼ cup finely chopped pecans*
*¼ cup firmly packed brown sugar*
*3 tablespoons all-purpose flour*
*1 teaspoon ground cinnamon*
*1 tablespoon butter or margarine*

Wash potatoes. Pat dry. Place on baking sheet and bake at 375 degrees for 1 hour or until done. Let cool slightly, peel, and mash. Stir in ⅓ cup brown sugar, orange juice, egg substitute, pumpkin pie spice, butter flavoring, orange peel, and salt. Spray 2-quart casserole with vegetable cooking spray. Spoon mixture into casserole. Set aside. Combine pecans, ¼ cup brown sugar, flour, and cinnamon. Cut in butter. Sprinkle over sweet potatoes. Bake at 350 degrees for 40 minutes.

# CARROT-CAULIFLOWER CASSEROLE

2 cups sliced cooked carrots
2 cups cauliflower flowerets, underdone
1⅓ cups plain croutons
1 cup grated Cheddar cheese
2 eggs, beaten
½ cup light cream
¼ cup melted butter
1 teaspoon Worcestershire sauce
1 teaspoon salt
½ teaspoon black pepper

Cook carrots and flowerets separately. Do not overcook. Place vegetables in buttered casserole. Stir in croutons and cheese. Mix eggs, cream, melted butter, and flavorings together and pour over vegetables. Bake at 350 degrees for ½ hour or until nicely browned.

# PUMPKIN DESSERT

*1 cup all-purpose flour*
*½ cup old-fashioned rolled oats*
*½ cup firmly packed brown sugar*
*½ cup butter or margarine, softened*
*¾ cup granulated sugar*
*1 16-ounce can pumpkin*
*1 12-ounce can evaporated milk*
*2 eggs*
*1 teaspoon cinnamon*
*¼ teaspoon salt*
*½ teaspoon ginger*
*¼ teaspoon cloves*
*½ cup firmly packed brown sugar*
*½ cup chopped pecans*
*Sweetened whipped cream*

Heat oven to 350 degrees. In small bowl, combine flour, rolled oats, ½ cup brown sugar, and butter. Beat at low speed, scraping bowl often until crumbly (1–2 minutes). Press mixture on bottom of 13×9–inch baking pan. Bake for 15 minutes.

While crust is baking, combine in large bowl granulated sugar, pumpkin, evaporated milk, eggs, cinnamon, salt, ginger, and cloves. Beat at medium speed, scraping bowl often, until smooth. Pour over crust; continue baking for 20 minutes.

In small bowl, stir together ½ cup brown sugar and pecans. Sprinkle over filling. Continue baking 15–20

minutes or until filling is firm to the touch or knife inserted in center comes out clean. Cool completely. Cut into squares. Store in refrigerator.

Serve with sweetened whipped cream.

# IRIS HOUSE B & B MYSTERIES
## by
## JEAN HAGER

### Featuring Proprietress and part-time sleuth, Tess Darcy

## THE LAST NOEL
### 78637-0/$5.50 US/$7.50 Can

When an out-of-town drama professor who was hired to direct the anual church Christmas pageant turns up dead, it's up to Tess to figure out who would be willing to commit a deadly sin on sacred grounds.

## DEATH ON THE DRUNKARD'S PATH
### 77211-6/$5.50 US/$7.50 Can

## DEAD AND BURIED
### 77210-8/$5.50 US/$7.50 Can

## A BLOOMING MURDER
### 77209-4/$5.50 US/$7.50 Can

# Murder Is on the Menu at the Hillside Manor Inn

Bed-and-Breakfast Mysteries by
## MARY DAHEIM
### featuring Judith McMonigle

**BANTAM OF THE OPERA**
76934-4/ $5.99 US/ $7.99 Can

**JUST DESSERTS**  76295-1/ $5.99 US/ $7.99 Can

**FOWL PREY**  76296-X/ $5.99 US/ $7.99 Can

**HOLY TERRORS**  76297-8/ $5.99 US/ $7.99 Can

**DUNE TO DEATH**  76933-6/ $5.99 US/ $7.99 Can

**A FIT OF TEMPERA**  77490-9/ $5.99 US/ $7.99 Can

**MAJOR VICES**  77491-7/ $5.99 US/ $7.99 Can

**MURDER, MY SUITE**
77877-7/ $5.99 US/ $7.99 Can

**AUNTIE MAYHEM**  77878-5/ $5.50 US/ $7.50 Can

**NUTTY AS A FRUITCAKE**
77879-3/ $5.99 US/ $7.99 Can

**SEPTEMBER MOURN**
78518-8/ $5.99 US/ $7.99 Can

# DEN OF ANTIQUITY MYSTERIES

## by
## TAMAR MYERS

### LARCENY AND OLD LACE
78239-1/$5.50 US/$7.50 Can

As owner of the Den of Antiquity, Abigail Timberlake
is accustomed to navigating the cutthroat world of rival
dealers at flea markets and auctions. But she never thought
she'd be putting her expertise in mayhem and detection to
other use—until her aunt was found murdered . . .

### GILT BY ASSOCIATION
78237-5/$5.50 US/$7.50 Can

A superb gilt-edged, 18th-century French armoire Abigail
purchased for a song at estate auction has just arrived
along with something she didn't pay for: a dead body.

### THE MING AND I
79255-9/$5.50 US/$7.50 Can

Digging up old family dirt can uncover long buried
secrets . . . and a new reason for murder.

If you and/or a friend would like to receive the *ROC Advance*, a bimonthly newsletter featuring all the newest and hottest ROC books and authors, on a complimentary basis, please fill out this form and return it to:

**ROC Books/Penguin USA**
375 Hudson Street
New York, NY 10014


Your Address
Name _____
Street _____ Apt. # _____
City _____ State _____ Zip _____

Friend's Address
Name _____
Street _____ Apt. # _____
City _____ State _____ Zip _____

# FLIGHTS OF FANTASY

**Buy them at your local**

**bookstore or use coupon**

**on next page for ordering.**

## About the Author

Robert Anton Wilson, in addition to being the author of more than twenty books, including *Sex and Drugs*, *Quantum Psychology*, *The Illuminatus Trilogy*, *The Schordinger's Cat Trilogy*, and *Prometheus Rising*, is a former *Playboy* editor, a philosopher, and a well-known lecturer. For information on his lectures and seminars, write PO Box 700305, San Jose, CA 95170.